7/4/85

Dear Gary,

I thought you
might enjoy this
bizarre little
exploration of
BLUEBEARD personal reality.

- - -

Best

BLUEBEARD

A Tale

MAX FRISCH

Translated from the German
by Geoffrey Skelton

A Harvest/HBJ Book
A Helen and Kurt Wolff Book
Harcourt Brace Jovanovich, Publishers
San Diego New York London

Requests for permission to make copies of any
part of the work should be mailed to: Permissions,
Harcourt Brace Jovanovich, Publishers,
Orlando, Florida 32887.

Library of Congress Cataloging in Publication Data
Frisch, Max, 1911–
Bluebeard: a tale.
Translation of: Blaubart.
"A Helen and Kurt Wolff book."
I. Title.
PT2611.R814B5613   1983   833'.912   82-21250
ISBN 0-15-113200-3
ISBN 0-15-613198-6 (pbk.)

Designed by Amy Hill
Printed in the United States of America
First Harvest/HBJ Edition 1984

A B C D E F G H I J

BLUEBEARD

— Do you recognize this tie, Herr Schaad?

— It has already been shown to me.

— This is the tie used in the strangling, as you know; presumably the victim was already suffocated, but clearly the murderer did not think the sanitary napkin in her mouth was enough, so he also used this tie.

— I am not the murderer.

— You understand my question?

— Yes.

— Is this your tie, or is it not?

— It could be. . . .

— Yes or no?

— As I've said already, I felt completely at home in her apartment, so maybe on some occasion I took my tie off because the weather was hot. That's conceivable. I was never in her apartment except during the day. As I've said already. And then maybe I forgot it, my tie, it's quite possible. I don't always wear a tie to go out, and so it got left in her apartment.

— Herr Doktor Schaad . . .
— That's conceivable.
— We have the forensic experts' report, and it leaves no room for doubt, Herr Doktor Schaad: it is your tie.

Acquitted because of insufficient evidence—
How does one live with that?
I am fifty-four years old.

 — So, Herr Schaad, you don't remember, and you still cannot say, where you were that Saturday afternoon when Rosalinde Z. was strangled with your tie in her apartment on the Hornstrasse. . .

What helps is billiards. I no longer stab with my cue, but strike gently and precisely, making the ball really roll. The hand becomes steadier when one plays every evening, and one's self-confidence increases, the coolness essential to the meticulous execution of some bold idea. I already achieve breaks of three or four shots. It is only when I miss and it is my opponent's turn, when I stand beside the green table waiting for my opponent to miss, it is only then that I hear the prosecutor again as I rub the blue chalk on my cue:

 — When you heard from your former assistant that Rosalinde Z. had been murdered on Satur-

day—that was of course on Monday, when you
went to your consulting room, pretending to
know nothing about it—

— There are no newspapers on Sunday.

— And that is why you knew nothing about it?

— Correct.

— Why then, Herr Doktor Schaad, did you immediately ask your assistant whether Rosalinde Z.
had been strangled?

— That was my first assumption.

— Why strangled?

— Prostitutes are usually strangled.

One can also play billiards by oneself. When I have
missed a shot, so that it is my opponent's turn, and I
have no opponent, I flick the three balls at random
with my fingers, blindly, and so violently that they
collide; I let chance take the place of an opponent. I
don't cheat, no point in that; I accept the position as
it is when the balls finally come to rest.

— Why tell lies? Nothing you have said, Herr
Doktor Schaad, provides an alibi. Why don't
you just confess?

When I see where my ball should go, and when I
take aim with the cue, my hand, the left one, which
doesn't have to strike but simply supports the strik-
ing cue, remains completely steady.

— Why didn't you go to the funeral Herr Doktor Schaad? There was no emergency call to prevent you. Not even that is true. You stayed in your consulting room and examined a mild case of hepatitis, and in between you had a lengthy telephone conversation with a travel agency. Is it not curious, Herr Doktor Schaad, that although you were in Zurich on that day, you did not put in an appearance at the funeral? After all, Rosalinde Z. had once been your wife. . . .

Now and again, when I can't get anything right, not even a simple carom, I change cues. Perhaps the cue is the trouble; there are short ones and long ones. But before I can bend over the green table once more and take aim, I have to chalk the new cue, and a pause ensues, letting the prosecutor in again:

— Regarding your regular visits to Rosalinde Z.: you knew what trade she was practicing in that apartment?
— Yes.
— And it didn't bother you?
— No.
— Is it correct, Herr Doktor Schaad, that while you were married to Rosalinde you were distressed when she so much as danced with another man? Not to mention the time when she sat up with her sick mother until midnight, in-

stead of returning home. Your extravagant jealousy is well known to a wide circle of friends. As one witness has put it: you were as wretched as a dog.

— While I was married to her, maybe . . .

— But not afterward?

— No.

— Did you know what kind of men frequented her apartment?

— That was her professional secret.

— But you did know, Herr Doktor Schaad, that Rosalinde Z. had nighttime clients, and that didn't distress you at all?

— No.

— How do you explain that?

— We had become friends.

— You had become friends. . . .

— I no longer had to rely on guesswork.

It is not enough to win the next shot by the simplest method that presents itself. You have to consider what the position of the three balls will be after the shot has been made. A maneuver off two cushions is risky, but if it succeeds, the stroke following is almost certain.

— So you frequently saw the accused, Herr Bickel. Did you also see other visitors in the hallway?

— I only work during the day.

— Did you ever see men leaving the house in the morning, when you were at work? If so, can you remember any of these men whom you came to recognize, even if you did not know them by name?

— I'm not employed as a watchman. . . .

— All the same, you have eyes.

— All I can say is I never bothered my head about it. When Madame Zogg went to the mailbox, she always greeted me. I work as a caretaker in other houses, too, and it's also happened there that a gentleman who is not a tenant leaves the house in the morning, and later if the lady is with her husband, she acts as if I were invisible. I don't know what you are getting at.

— So you have seen the accused. . . .

— In the daytime, now and then, yes.

— Did you see him on that Saturday?

— No.

— Herr Bickel, you are contradicting the first statement you made to the police. You said then that Herr Schaad had been unable to use the elevator that Saturday and had walked up the stairs.

— My wife saw him.

— You did not see him yourself?

— I said I was down in the basement.

— So you cannot say whether the accused, when he walked up the stairs that Saturday because the elevator was not running, had flowers in his hand, such as lilies?

— No.

— You were working in the basement. . . .

— That's what I keep saying: the elevator was not running because I had to oil the doors, and that's why I was in the basement.

— When was that, Herr Bickel?

— Between eleven and twelve.

— After that the elevator was running again?

— Of course.

— Another question, Herr Bickel . . .

— It wasn't just that I had to oil the doors; I also removed those scrawls that keep appearing in the elevator, and that takes time—nowadays it isn't just chalk or felt-tip marker.

— What is it, then?

— Spray paint.

— I see. . . .

— JESUS RULES.

— A final question, Herr Bickel . . .

— That's all been stopped now.

— Did you notice whether the accused had a key to Rosalinde Z.'s mailbox, or whether he ever tried in any way to extract letters from her box?

— Herr Doktor Schaad is a gentleman.

I can no longer feed the swans.
Their long necks—

After I have scattered a few crumbs (my breakfast rolls) on the water, they come gliding up in a leisurely way, as always, bending their long necks and snapping without greed or haste. Whether, after my ten months in detention on remand, they are the same swans I fed before, I do not know. They stretch up their long necks again. They do not recognize me, and move off somewhere else.

— The prosecutor will address the court.

Swans are not witnesses.

— For the last time, Herr Doktor Schaad, I ask you where you were after you left Rosalinde Z. around noon, on, as you maintain, the best of terms.
— Maybe I fed the swans.
— Swans?
— Yes.
— Did you often feed swans?
— From time to time.
— Where?
— At the lake.
— Wasn't it raining or snowing on that Saturday?
— That doesn't worry the swans.

During the day in the consulting room when nobody is waiting, no emergency call to answer, as I sit

there in my white coat with my feet on the desk, it
continues:

— At the preliminary hearing you claimed to have
gone for a walk on the Saturday in question,
and you even named the place, Wasberg or
something like that. As a rule, you said, you
leave your car near the gravel pit, then walk
through the woods, sometimes not knowing
exactly where you are: there are these logging
paths leading nowhere. . . . Unfortunately, it
turns out that on this Saturday your blue
Volvo was not at the gravel pit, Herr Doktor
Schaad, but in the garage on the Kreuzplatz.
— I admitted my mistake. . . .
— Whereupon you claimed that you were in your
consulting room, though your office is closed
on Saturdays. You went there to search for tax
documents. And you also gave us the exact
time: between three-thirty and five in the afternoon.
— Yes.
— Around this time, Rosalinde Z. was strangled
in her apartment. . . . Unfortunately, your former assistant, who was working on that Saturday, did not see you in your office, nor did she
hear you. Eventually, you retracted the assertion about having been in your consulting
room in order to fetch tax documents at the

9

time in question in favor of a Czech film, which you alleged you were watching at the time Rosalinde Z. was murdered. Your description of the film shows that you have a remarkable memory, Herr Doktor Schaad, for it turns out that this particular Czech film has not been shown anywhere in the past eighteen months. . . . Only your fourth assertion—that you bought some tobacco en route, namely on the Feldeggstrasse—has to some extent been confirmed. The place where you bought this tobacco is not very far from the scene of the crime. . . .

Actually, I might just as well close my practice down. Now and again there are emergency cases—that is to say, patients who cannot choose their doctor—or a house call to be made at night. During the day the waiting room is empty; my assistant, the new one, files the professional journals. It is possible that one or two of my long-time patients have died while I was in detention, and others were obliged to change doctors, which is understandable: ten months is a long time. The coat I put on each morning when I come to the office is as white as ever. One patient, after sitting alone in the waiting room for the third time, gradually loses confidence; he looks relieved when I finally refer him to a urologist, and after that I read the old magazines lying in the waiting room. I now have more time than ever before. Even on the day of my arrest, the waiting room was so crowded they were sitting on the window sill. People know of my acquittal, but they also know too much about me personally. It was difficult to find a new assistant. This one comes from Yugoslavia. She has to knock before she enters my consulting room; I do not wish my assistant to see me with my feet on the desk, my hands clasped behind my neck. The few patients who continue to respect my medical skill are apparently in good health at the moment, and I might just as well sit at home. Nobody calls me at home, either. One or two, who were witnesses at my trial and clearly did not expect an acquittal, seem embarrassed by the thought of seeing me again.

— Is it true, Herr Pfeifer, that you once heard the accused say he could strangle this woman?
— He'd had a lot to drink.
— But you did hear him say that?

The witness blows his nose.

— How long have you been friends with Felix Schaad?
— I've never slept with his Rosalinde!
— That was not my question.
— Maybe that's what he thought. . . .

— And that's why he wanted to strangle Rosa-
  linde?
— I found her charming.
— Another question, Herr Pfeifer . . .
— As a hostess, I mean.
— With regard to the loan—
— He insisted I should never mention it. He
  helped me complete my studies. Why should I
  deny it? Anyway, it wasn't a loan. When I
  asked him for one at the time, he refused, say-
  ing he did not make loans. Loans are a strain on
  friendship, he said.
— How large a sum was it?
— Twenty-five thousand, I believe . . .

The witness blows his nose.

— I don't know what you expect me to say. . . .
— So you often spent the night at the Schaads'?
— I don't deny that.
— You heard the accused say he could strangle
  this woman. Or do you deny, Herr Pfeifer, that
  you frequently repeated that story among your
  common circle of acquaintances?

When I have been to the toilet and am washing my
hands, I still have the feeling that, as soon as I have
dried my hands, I shall return to the courtroom to
listen to the next witness.

— You are Frau Bickel?
— Yes.
— First name?
— Isolde.
— Your profession?
— Cleaning lady.
— Your duty as a witness, Frau Bickel, is to tell the truth and nothing but the truth; you are aware that perjury carries a prison sentence—in aggravated cases, up to five years' penal servitude. . . .

There are probably witnesses who expect me to send them a note thanking them for what they said in court.

— I can only say that the doctor is a person who wouldn't hurt a fly; that's all I can say.

Three weeks after my acquittal, I still have not written a single letter, I am still sitting there with folded arms, as in court.

— So, Frau Bickel, you were frequently in her apartment when Madame was alone, to do the cleaning, and, if I understand you correctly, that was in the mornings?
— Sometimes the doctor was there as well.
— You saw no other gentlemen?

— Only in the hallway . . . Sometimes she also wanted me there in the evenings. When she had a lot of guests. And they weren't just gentlemen, you know—married couples, too—and there was always a lot of talking. Usually with a cold buffet. I don't know what sort of people they were, but Frau Rosalinde was always the center of attention, you could sense that.

— On these occasions Herr Doktor Schaad was not present?

— No.

— You remember no names?

— One of them was a Greek; he was actually staying there for a while, a student, bald, but with a black beard. Sometimes he would come into the kitchen, but he couldn't speak German, and he always looked so solemn. Somehow I felt sorry for him. I think he didn't like all that company, so he kept coming into the kitchen to get a drink of water.

— Anything else?

— Nothing else I can think of, really.

— At the preliminary hearing, Frau Bickel, you said that on the Saturday on which Frau Rosalinde was murdered, the elevator was not running.

— That happens sometimes.

— And that Herr Schaad walked up the stairs.

— There was nothing else he could do.

— And what time was that?
— Between eleven and twelve.
— So you saw Herr Schaad?
— The elevator is often out of order; maybe the door gets stuck, or the light in the cage goes off again—you'll have to ask my husband, he's the caretaker.
— Your husband saw nobody.
— Because he was working in the basement.
— When did you leave the house, Frau Bickel?
— Shortly after twelve.
— When did Herr Schaad leave the house?
— I don't know.
— But you were in the hallway, I believe.
— By then the elevator was working again.
— After Herr Schaad had gone up the stairs, did you hear quarreling on the fourth floor, more like shouting?
— I was cleaning on the second floor.
— You heard nothing?
— I always clean from upstairs to downstairs.
— You knew that Herr Doktor Schaad and Frau Rosalinde had at one time been married, or did you only learn that later, at the preliminary hearing?
— I had a feeling, somehow.
— One last question, Frau Bickel . . .
— He never brought her champagne.
— Why did you go back to the Hornstrasse that

Saturday evening? At the first hearing you said it had been prearranged. . . .

— Yes; otherwise I wouldn't have gone.

— What was prearranged, Frau Bickel?

— For me to help her pack and do the ironing.

— Frau Rosalinde was going away?

— Apparently.

— When you called the police, you were very confused, Frau Bickel, understandably so; at the preliminary hearing you could not say whether the front door to the apartment was locked or not. . . .

— I think it was locked.

— Which would mean that the murderer had a key to the apartment, and that is very important, Frau Bickel.

— Yes.

— So you think the door was locked?

— I don't know.

What helps is billiards.

— It may be, as we have heard tell, that the accused is a person who wouldn't hurt a fly. Unfortunately, in this case we are not dealing with a fly. . . .

Sometimes the presiding judge helps:

— Herr Prosecutor, I must ask you not to speak in
   that tone of voice.

When I am playing billiards by myself, sometimes
the pause after I have missed a shot takes too much
time; I stand at the table, rub blue chalk on my cue
as I study the new position of the balls, and rub and
rub; there is no opponent waiting impatiently for
me to point my cue and play on; I stand and rub and
hear my defense attorney:

— So it would be true to say, Herr Schaad, that
   you knew, if only vaguely, about this woman's
   past?
— I loved her.
— That was not my question, Herr Schaad.
— I loved her.
— So you have already said.
— I loved her.
— You knew, then: marriage at the age of nine-
   teen, because an officer, an air force captain,
   had raped her. Her father was a major and a
   cantonal councilor. A hopeless marriage from
   the very start. Which was the reason why she
   started a clandestine love affair after only a few
   months. Her first love. That was in Sion. The
   captain sued on grounds of adultery, and after
   the divorce she went to Bern to study.
— For a term or two.

— What else did you know?

— That she lacked self-confidence.

— Can you put that more explicitly?

— Her father the major had expectations for her that she was simply unable to fulfill, and as a result Rosalinde lost all trust in herself. Only as a woman, I believe, did she always enjoy success, and she needed that as self-affirmation. That is easy enough to understand. All I know is that in Bern she lived with a man whom she really loved, for three or five years. A singer. I have forgotten his name.

— It says here a commercial artist.

— The commercial artist was her second husband. The singer was married, often away on tours, and almost ten years older than Rosalinde.

— What else did you know?

— She was not a nymphomaniac.

— But from time to time she needed self-affirmation as a woman, because her father the major in Sion had other expectations for her, and all of that you could understand, Herr Doktor Schaad. . . .

— Yes.

— Is it correct, Herr Schaad, that you had a secret relationship with Rosalinde while she was married to the commercial artist?

— Yes.

— That was in Bern.

— Yes.

— While you had a wife in Zurich.
— Yes.
— Do you know how the commercial artist in
  Bern took it when he heard of her clandestine
  affair, I mean her affair with you?
— It came as a shock to him, I believe.
— Did Rosalinde talk about it?
— In a way, yes, not precisely.
— What precisely did you know?
— She was not a nymphomaniac. . . .
— You have told us that already.
— Basically she is a friend, a comrade.
— And that is what led to your sixth marriage.
— That is the truth.
— When you were eventually married to Rosa-
  linde, Herr Doktor Schaad, and when one
  morning at breakfast you demanded to know
  what had been going on for the past six
  months, how did you take it, Herr Doktor
  Schaad?
— You mean her affair with Jan. . . .
— For instance.
— That had been going on for more than a year.
— Were you surprised?
— Yes.
— You were surprised. . . .

When I am playing billiards by myself, there are
occasionally onlookers waiting, glass in hand, to see
how I intend to tackle my next move. That forces me

19

to play on, which is why I welcome such onlookers. Usually they do not stay long; when I have played and missed two or three times, I find myself alone again.

— The prosecutor will address the court. . . .

He will never be convinced by my acquittal.

— As for the locking arrangements, let me summarize: a forcible entry into the apartment has to be ruled out. There are no traces of damage. So there remain two possible alternatives. One is that the spring lock was opened from the inside, which means that Rosalinde Z. let the murderer into her apartment. This is contradicted, however, by the fact that at the time in question Rosalinde Z., as we have heard, was under the influence of a strong sedative. Which is the reason, presumably, why there was no resistance. The second possibility: that the murderer was in possession of a key to the apartment. We do not know who, apart from the accused and the cleaning lady, possessed a key; but it is beyond all doubt that the accused possessed a key.

What was not disclosed in court: our former boyhood games in the gravel pit. Little Egon, whose feet we had fettered because no red Indian can be named Egon, was found three days later by a police dog. He was suffering from pneumonia (he did not dare tell at the time who had fettered him), and later, as a well-known pianist, he died in an air crash; beyond reach as a witness.

— As his assistant, you, too, Fräulein Schlegel, would confirm that in human terms the accused, unless his medical duties demand otherwise, is a person who would not hurt a fly. . . .

The gravel pit, where a group of boy scouts assembled while Rosalinde Z. was lying strangled in her apartment, and where my blue Volvo was not seen, a gravel pit like any other, lies, as I maintained during the first hearing, between Zumikon and Ebmatingen.
This the police confirmed.
I am grateful for each and every confirmation.

— So you were at the doctor's office, Fräulein Schlegel, although it was a Saturday, doing some work, and you say you did not leave the office the whole afternoon. . .
— I was waiting for a telephone call.
— And in order not to miss this telephone call, you did not go out all afternoon, not to drink coffee, for example, or to buy cigarettes. . . .

— I don't smoke.
— I am asking you now for the last time . . .
— I was working in the laboratory at the back, and from there I can't see anyone who might be passing through the hallway. Besides, the doctor has a key; he doesn't need to ring the bell when he arrives.
— So you did not see the accused?
— I am not saying I did. . . .
— Did you hear the accused?

The witness reflects.

— Fräulein Schlegel, your duty is to tell the truth.
— Perhaps he went through the hallway just as my friend was calling me and didn't want to interrupt me, so he went into his consulting room; yes, I think that is possible.
— What time did your friend call you?
— Soon after four, I think.
— At what time did you leave the office?
— Shortly before five, I think.
— Without having seen the accused . . .

The witness is silent.

— I have no further questions to ask this witness.

The prosecutor leans back.

The witness looks frightened.

The defense attorney rises:

— When you are working in this laboratory at the back, Fräulein Schlegel, can you hear anyone cough, for example, in the consulting room, or can you hear anything else, such as footsteps?
— No.
— Why not?
— Because it has wall-to-wall carpeting.

The photographs, taken by the police forensic department: the nakedness of the corpse in the morgue, the vagina covered by a black strip, a significant feature the blue weals on the victim's neck; an enlargement of these; significant, too, the ankles bound together; an enlargement shows that the murderer first secured the victim's feet with adhesive tape. Why was there evidently no struggle on the victim's part? That is significant in that there were no scratch marks to be found on Felix Schaad, arrested five days after the murder. The third enlargement: the sanitary napkin in the victim's mouth; in all probability this had caused her suffocation, and the murderer had no need to strangle her with the tie besides. Finally, the photograph the prosecutor is calling for at this moment: the victim on the carpet beside the bed, fully clothed, her hands laid in her lap, on her breast the five lilies.

— What can be said with complete certainty is that we are dealing here with a crime of passion. Robbery with homicidal assault can be ruled out, as I explained earlier. The procedure the murderer used, suffocating his victim with a sanitary napkin, suggests jealousy as a motive. . . .

Walking helps for a while.

— Why are you trudging through underbrush?
— Because the path has suddenly given out.
— Why has the path given out?
— A logging path . . .
— You know this wood, you claim, so why don't you keep to the paths you have known for years on end, Herr Doktor Schaad, particularly on a foggy day like this?
— I dislike walking on asphalt.
— You like underbrush. . . .
— Not necessarily, no, not when it is wet like today and when you are walking in ordinary shoes that keep slipping.
— What do you mean by a logging path?
— One doesn't always recognize it from the start. It begins as a regular path, wide enough, and sometimes one is walking on gravel: farther on there is no more gravel, but still a path of sorts. Between felled tree trunks. The trunks, I be-

lieve, had been stripped. And suddenly, in a clearing, there are just these deep bulldozer tracks, curves in the mud; the rest is underbrush.

— Have you seen any forestry workers?
— No.
— Have you heard a chain saw?
— No.
— So you would assume, Herr Doktor Schaad, that for about one hour you have been seen by nobody?
— I wouldn't know.
— Do you know where you are at this moment?
— Above Toggwil . . .
— Why do you choose these particular cobwebs to piss on?

Later I feel the need for a beer, a snack.

— When the gentleman came into the bar, was he wearing a tie? And if so, do you recall the color of his tie?

The waitress reflects.

— You no longer know. . . .
— No.
— Did you recognize the gentleman?
— I've only been here a month.

— And you know nothing about the Schaad case?

— No.

— What did you notice about him?

The witness reflects.

— Didn't you notice anything at all?

— He put his hand on the green tile stove, I did notice that, and then he wanted the seat next to the stove, which is usually held for regular guests, and I noticed the gentleman hadn't had a shave, I think, and he didn't take off his cap, yes, it was a sort of beret.

— Did he seem on edge?

— When I gave him the short menu, he didn't even look at me, but right away ordered a small beer.

— And then what happened?

— He just sat there by the stove.

— Weren't you surprised when he asked you your name and later wrote it down on a scrap of paper?

— Did he do that?

— So you didn't notice. . . .

— When I brought his beer he ordered a bratwurst, which we don't serve at that time of day. He didn't seem to have read our short menu. After two o'clock we serve only cold dishes, salami, things like that.

— So this was after two o'clock. . . .

— I'm sure of that.

— Did the gentleman talk with you?

— I did notice the gentleman kept looking at me when I was at the buffet, but waitresses are used to that. Maybe he said something about the weather. I've long since stopped listening when they talk about the weather, since I don't go walking myself.

— Was there anything else that caught your attention?

— I had the glasses to wipe.

— How long did he stay?

— Later on he ordered a schnapps.

— At what time was that?

— A quarter to four.

— How do you know that so exactly?

— Because the gentleman suddenly asked what time it was, though we've got a clock over the buffet and he himself had a wristwatch. So why did he have to ask? That did strike me as a bit strange.

— And he said nothing else?

— When he stood up after paying, I said good-bye, as I always do, and he said: It's now a quarter past five, miss, a quarter past five exactly, as if it was important for me to know that. . . .

— Did he drink more than one schnapps?

— Three.

— What effect did they have on him?
— He was sweating.
— What else did you notice?

The witness reflects.

— Was he talking to himself?
— He asked where the telephone was.
— And did he go to the telephone?
— Not right away. . . .
— And what happened next?
— Then he suddenly got up.
— How long was he telephoning?
— He didn't get through, he said, and that was true—we can see by the meter—but later the gentleman went back to the booth, then once more, and he said the line was busy.

The truth and nothing but the truth.

— Herr Schaad, whom were you trying just now to call from this restaurant?
— Rosalinde.
— And the number was busy?
— I was told it had been disconnected.
— It is a year today since Rosalinde Z. was murdered, and you were surprised, Herr Doktor Schaad, that this number was no longer in service?

— No.
— All the same, you tried it several times?
— Three times. . . .

What is also no help: alcohol.

— Have you often seen him intoxicated?
— It has happened.
— What was his behavior?
— I'd rather not say. . . .
— Did he become aggressive, for instance?
— Melancholy.
— You mean he became tearful. . . .
— I didn't say that.
— He felt sorry for himself, you mean.
— I don't believe Papa is a murderer, I don't be-
  lieve it. An egoist, yes, he is that. The way he
  treated my mother . . . well, I was only a child at
  the time . . . and what my mother told me now
  and again, she can tell you herself. And how do
  I know how she treated him? Now I'm sixteen,
  and I don't believe everything I'm told.
— What do you mean by the word egoist?
— I really meant egocentric.
— Is there a difference?
— An egoist gives nothing.
— And that was not the case with your papa?
— No, goodness, no.
— And what about an egocentric?

— He'd sooner kill himself first.
— If he weren't a coward.
— I didn't say that.

The witness sobs.

— I can't be expected to describe my own father!

Three weeks after my acquittal I am still being de-
fended, wherever I am, walking, lying, or standing;
at this moment I am sitting in a sauna, my elbows on
my knees, my hands covering my face.

— Regarding the microscopic traces on the tie, we
are told by the experts that this is pipe tobacco,
and if I have understood you correctly, Professor, all the articles of clothing belonging
to the accused contain microscopic traces of tobacco, even after they have been to the
cleaners. . . .
— That is right.
— But the accused has never denied that the tie
used by the murderer was his tie, so I don't
understand what this expert testimony is sup-
posed to prove.
— I do not wish to be misunderstood. . . .
— Must the murderer be a pipe smoker?
— As I said, it is a matter of microscopic traces
which we have analyzed and identified beyond

doubt. Unfortunately, the particles on the tie used in the strangulation are much too small, and we cannot say for certain that they represent the brand of tobacco the accused usually smokes.

— You understood my question?

— I can only repeat what is in our report; you have heard this report, and you will also be receiving it in writing.

— Why don't you answer my question?

— On the basis of our scientific analysis, the accused, who leaves microscopic traces of tobacco everywhere, cannot be ruled out as the murderer.

— That is obvious.

— What was your question?

— It seems to me important, on the other hand, to know where else, apart from the tie, microscopic traces of tobacco were found. . . .

— That is indicated in our report.

— If I heard correctly: on the towel in the bathroom, on the armrest of an easy chair, but not on Rosalinde Z.'s bed linen; on the other hand, here and there in the kitchen and on the left sleeve of her overcoat, virtually everywhere, in fact, but not on the corpse, if I heard you correctly, not on the dress she was wearing. And hence my question: how does the expert witness explain the fact that microscopic traces pointing to the accused can be found almost everywhere in the apartment except on the victim herself? . . . Maybe Herr Schaad did not smoke on this particular day, his hands were as clean as when he is working in his consulting room or at the hospital. What, then, do these traces of tobacco prove—that the tie was once his, yes; and what else?

— I refer you to our report.

— I have already heard it, Professor.

— As I believe I have already explained, it depends on the material—for example, a very smooth silk in contrast to a woolen tie of the kind used by the murderer, or a linen towel or the tapestry of an easy chair, and so on. Very smooth silk is one of the least satisfactory materials for purposes of microscopic traces, likewise for fingerprints, as I believe I mentioned in the report, while the wool of a tie, though advantageous for tobacco traces, is not any better for fingerprints than silk is, and everything has been done to secure fingerprints on the scene of the crime. Also, I have never maintained that the fingerprints on the murdered woman's leather coat and in her apartment belong exclusively to Herr Doktor Schaad, and to return to the tobacco traces, these have indeed not been discovered on the victim herself, but they have on the carpet on which the victim was lying, and in copious amounts, as I said. It is not a question of cigarette ash, though there is that, too, but we know that cigarette tobacco burns away either completely or not at all, whereas a mixture of ash and half-burnt tobacco, even when present only in microscopic particles, is attributable to pipe tobacco. Indeed, beyond all doubt.

Taking photographs is not allowed in court; the newspapers print only sketches: the accused with folded arms, looking up at the ceiling.

— You are Frau Schaad?
— Yes.
— Your first name?
— Lilian.
— Your maiden name was Habersack.
— That is correct.
— Occupation?
— Nursery-school teacher.
— You are divorced, Frau Schaad?
— That is correct.
— So you know the accused personally. . . .

Laughter in court.

— Your duty as a witness is to tell the truth and nothing but the truth; you are aware that perjury carries a prison sentence—in aggravated cases, up to five years' penal servitude.

When wives are being questioned the courtroom is full; marriage, even for young people, still seems to be a problem.

— When you were married to him, did the accused physically assault you, or threaten to do so? At times of tension did he, for example, slap your face or take you by the throat, causing you to fear strangulation?

In the sauna there is no need to talk, everyone sits there naked and sweats; in fact, people do not even look at one another until they go to the shower and then into the open to cool off.

— Would it therefore be correct, Frau Doktor, to say that though the accused did not become violent, he tends to be jealous, and this distressed you, especially since he had absolutely no grounds for jealousy?

The witness nods.

— And in what manner did his almost pathological jealousy reveal itself?

The witness reflects.

— Did he open letters?
— I don't think so.
— Yet all the same he didn't trust you. . . .
— For instance, he would send me flowers. With no indication of who sent them. And when I unwrapped them, he would watch me, trying to see if the flowers made me embarrassed.

I am still sitting there steaming, I place my blue towel over my belly as the state-appointed defense attorney takes the floor. I feel more naked than the others steaming alongside me.

— Is it correct, Frau Doktor Schaad, that after the divorce you stayed on friendly terms with the accused?
— Why not?
— Can you recall the behavior of the accused when you last met him in the vegetarian restaurant to seek his advice on tax matters?
— He didn't give me any advice. . . .
— All the same, he met you, Frau Doktor Schaad, two days after the murder—that was on the Monday—and you did not get the impression that Herr Schaad was anticipating arrest?
— No.
— Did he seem on edge?

— I showed him the tax reminder, and he behaved
  as if it were no concern of his. . .
- What did he say, then?
— He was a bit odd, I have to admit.
— Not his usual self?
— He said he wasn't my permanent tax ad-
  viser. . . .
— You ate together?
— He didn't eat a thing.
— So he wasn't your permanent tax adviser; and
  what else did Herr Doktor Schaad tell you in
  this vegetarian restaurant?

The witness reflects.

— Did he mention Rosalinde Z.?
— Yes.
— Did you already know about the murder?
— No.
— You learned about it through him?
— Yes.
— And what did Herr Doktor Schaad have to say
  about it?
— He had tears in his eyes.

I shall change saunas. It is only bearable when nobody knows me, when the man in charge doesn't
greet me, when nobody watches me sweating and
dripping, my elbows on my knees, my eyes shut.

— You are likewise Frau Schaad?
— Yes.
— Your first name is Gisela?
— Gisel.
— Your maiden name was Stamm?
— That's right.
— You, too, were married to the accused and divorced, Frau Doktor Schaad, and are consequently familiar with the character of the accused. . . .

The witness nods.

— How long were you married?

The witness reflects.

— Approximately?
— We were living together when Schaad was still married, and later we got married, but we no longer lived together, not in that way; I don't quite know how to put it; he denies it was a marriage at all.
— Still, it's his name you are bearing.
— That's right.
— Your occupation?
— I was a medical assistant. . . .

Worse than anything wives can say in evidence are the memories the court does not hear about: the

gray rabbit (PINOCCHIO) under the razor, and how
little Felix cried for days after the rabbit was no
longer alive, his mama bought him another one but
he never loved it as much as the gray one.

— Is what the witness has just said correct, Herr
  Schaad?
— Our recollections conflict.
— The witness says you repeatedly threatened to
  leave her luggage on the platform and go on
  alone if she should ever again arrive late on the
  platform, and this in the very first year of your
  marriage.
— I don't remember that. . . .
— And on one occasion, Herr Doktor Schaad,
  three years later, that's what you actually did,
  the witness tells us: the witness intended only
  to go to the booth to buy cigarettes, and she ran
  into somebody, or looked at a window display,
  and when she returned to the platform, all her
  luggage was standing on the platform, and you,
  her husband, were waving from the moving
  train.
— That was in Bern.
— So you do remember that.
— Yes.
— Is it correct to say, Herr Doktor Schaad, that
  the moment things go contrary to your mas-
  culine wishes, you very quickly lose your
  temper?

It does no good for the accused to laugh. It does not put the witness at her ease; on the contrary, it is only the prosecutor who immediately profits:

— Is it true, Frau Doktor, that you occasionally spent the night with a lady friend, although, as you maintain, the accused never took you by the throat or in any other way physically threatened you?

— I don't understand the question. . . .

— Frau Doktor, why will you not admit that you sometimes spent the night with a lady friend because you were sometimes frightened of this man?

The defense attorney intervenes:

— Regarding the nights spent with a lady friend, I have a question to put to the accused: so you knew, Herr Schaad, where your former wife sometimes spent the night when she felt frightened of you?

— Yes.

— How did you know?

— She told me.

— Did you once ask this lady friend whether she also knew that your wife, when in distress, sometimes spent the night with her?

— I once called her, yes. . . .

— Because you doubted your wife's story.

— Because I was worried about her.

— And she was there, in distress?

— Yes.

— Did you speak to her?

— No.

— Why not?

— Her friend said my wife was already asleep and it was very late, which it was—it was nearly three in the morning—so I begged her pardon.

— You were relieved?

— I was drunk.

— And your wife found out. . . .

— Unfortunately, yes; I apparently talked a lot of nonsense, and my wife heard about it in the morning.

— After that you never telephoned again?

— No.

— On another occasion when your wife felt threatened at home by you, and for that reason spent the night with the afore-mentioned friend, you went to a concert in the Tonhalle and saw the afore-mentioned friend in the lobby. Is that correct?

— That is correct.

— What did you think of that?

— She was very embarrassed.

— And what did this friend have to say?

— We just nodded to each other.

What can be relied on to help, but only for a short time: the ergometer, which as a doctor one so often recommends. Most patients find it too boring. Ten minutes of stress with an eye on the wattage dial. Then the pulse rate subsides, and it goes on:

— You are likewise Frau Schaad?
— Yes.
— Your first name is Corinne.
— That's right.
— Your maiden name?
— Vogel.
— You are likewise divorced. . . .

It does no good for the accused when the jury sees that a witness is boring him; boredom conveys a hint of cruelty.

— So you, too, Frau Schaad, can recall no threats of physical violence; on the other hand, you were distressed by his habit of pacing the room and delivering lectures, as you call them, sometimes even after midnight. . . .
— Yes.
— Did that happen often?
— Two or three times a month.
— Can you tell us what the accused lectured you about as he paced the room?

The witness reflects.

— Did he insult you?
— That's not his way.
— What, then, did you perceive as cruel?
— I wanted to sleep. . . .
— So you no longer recall what Herr Doktor Schaad lectured you about for hours, keeping you from sleeping?
— Theory . . .
— Of what?
— He was trying to persuade me. . . .
— And he did not succeed?
— Once, when I was not listening, Felix hurled a cup against the wall; that did happen once.
— Because you were not listening?
— It wasn't a valuable cup.

The house on the Lindenstrasse in which the witness was assaulted, not physically but mentally, has in the meantime been demolished, which is a pity: an art-nouveau building. It must have happened some time ago; green is sprouting from the rubble behind the fence, ENTRY BY UNAUTHORIZED PERSONS STRICTLY PROHIBITED, even blossoms are pushing through the fence, and only the fireproof wall facing the house next door still shows where the floors once were, the staircase, the blue toilets one above the other; sparrows now flutter where once we lived.

— Is what the witness says correct, Herr Schaad?

There is no such thing as a common memory.
What helps is billiards.
I have now become so adept that, unless faced with a particularly difficult problem on the green rectangle beneath the lamp, I can go right on playing while I listen to yet another wife.

— You are likewise Frau Schaad?
— That is correct.
— Your first name?
— Andrea.
— Your maiden name?
— Padrutt.
— Your occupation is housewife.
— That is not correct.
— But it's entered here: housewife.
— At the moment I'm working in a gallery.
— What do you call such work?
— I was a graduate student. . . .
— Your duty as a witness, Frau Doktor, is to tell the truth and nothing but the truth; you are aware that perjury carries a prison sentence—in aggravated cases, up to five years' penal servitude.
— I studied Romance languages. . . .
— The prosecutor will question you first.

What still causes me trouble: the reverse spin or screw shot or whatever it is called; I am rarely successful with that.

— You understand the question, Frau Schaad?

— No.

— When you were married to him, did the accused threaten you physically? At times of tension, did he, for example, beat you with his fists or take you by the throat, causing you to fear strangulation?

I really must practice the screw shot: strike from above, hitting the ball in the lower half so that, when it collides with and is checked by the object ball, it is forced by its own spin to recoil. The stroke must be sharp but short, to keep the cue from damaging the green table. My first attempt fails. The second attempt fails, the third is successful but leaves my ball in a hopeless position, so that the fourth shot also misses; but then I pull off a whole run, without counting the winning shots, and the break is still in progress as I take up the blue chalk and rub my cue again.

— Can you give us an example, Frau Doktor? You say Felix Schaad is affectionate, but the possessive type. . . .

— Yes, that's what led to our divorce.

— Can you give an example of that?

The witness reflects.

— Perhaps it might help, Frau Schaad, if I remind you that at this time you had a relationship

with another man, who unfortunately was
married.

— I don't understand the question. . . .
— You accompanied him to congresses all over
the world, Frau Schaad, as his assistant, and
that was no secret; Felix Schaad knew about it.
— That was professional.
— What were you afraid of at the time?
— I don't understand the question. . . .
— When Herr Schaad wanted to know once
whether it was a love affair, you denied it, be-
cause, I assume, you were afraid of something.
— I didn't want to hurt him.
— You didn't want to hurt him. . . .
— That's right.
— Because you were afraid that the accused, when
he discovered what others already knew, would
be capable of anything, that he might, for in-
stance, take off his tie and strangle you on the
spot?
— I don't think he had it in him to do that.
— All the same, you were afraid of him?
— He can get very annoyed.
— Can you give us an example?

The witness reflects.

— At some later date, he learned from an outside
source that the reason you had been living with
him these three years was that Professor L. was

also married and, what's more, had children; when you more or less confirmed these facts, how did the accused react?

— He showed great self-control.

— In what way?

— He said nothing at all.

— For how long?

— For days, and then he went on a trip. . . .

— And a letter arrived from Vienna, a copy of which lies before the court; I don't know, Frau Schaad, whether you remember this rather lengthy letter?

— By then this affair, as he thought of it, was over.

— And what happened after that?

— From then on he slept in his studio.

— And what else?

— I was very depressed at that time.

— Because he was so possessive?

— Because he began drinking.

— And when he was drunk, Frau Schaad—and this is my final question—what did he do when he had too much to drink?

— He talked. . . .

— What about?

— Always the same thing . . .

— And that was?

— I can't remember.

— You can't remember. . . .

Sometimes the presiding judge has also had enough:

— Can the witness now be allowed to stand down?

The witness takes up her handbag.

— The trial is adjourned to Monday morning at eight.

I place my billiard cue back in the rack. I put on my jacket. I had not removed my tie for the game; I pull it tight. In the adjoining bar I order a Fernet-Branca. I stand there in my overcoat and cap. It is daylight outside. I look for my car. No ticket, though my parking meter has run out. I get in behind the steering wheel. It is raining. I insert the ignition key and ask myself where I am living at the moment.

— So, Herr Knüttel, you recall that he was in your shop and you spoke to him. Is that correct?
— Yes.
— He was interested in antiques. . . .
— That is correct.
— Was he looking for anything in particular?
— I had noticed the gentleman several times before; he would stand in front of my shop window, sometimes for as long as a quarter of an hour, even when it was raining; he had his eye on some particular object, that was my impression.
— Do you know what he had his eye on?

— No.
— For several weeks, Herr Doktor Schaad asserts,
you had an English writing desk, cherry with
green leather. . . .
— That is correct, yes, so I did.
— When Herr Schaad finally entered the shop to
inspect this English writing desk, did he ask
you the price?
— That is correct, yes, I remember now, but the
English writing desk had already been sold
when Herr Schaad came into the shop for the
first time and inquired about the price. It ap-
peared he had liked the piece.
— Do you still know from whom you acquired it?
— From a lady.
— From a Frau Doktor Schaad?
— That might be.
— Did the accused make any remark concerning
the English writing desk that had been sold, or
did he just look at it?
— He wanted to know the exact measurements.
— What for?
— I don't know. I took the measurements: the
writing desk was exactly the size the gentleman
had thought it to be.
— And then he left your shop?
— No.
— And?
— He looked around. . . . I had other writing

desks, but obviously not what the gentleman was looking for. Later he asked me whether he might also see the storeroom, and I showed it to him. He looked it over very thoroughly. A chair, a rocking chair, seemed to catch his interest. He sat down in it. When I said the chair was very comfortable, he laughed and said he knew that. And then he asked the price of a French grandfather clock.

— Which you had also acquired from the same lady?
— That's right.
— And what else?
— When I noticed that the gentleman was impressed by several pieces, I offered him a cup of tea, as I always do, and he didn't refuse it, but he didn't sit down to drink his tea, he stayed on his feet and said he felt as if he were at home in my storeroom.
— Did Herr Schaad come to see you again?
— No.

One is also questioned about dreams:

— So you had the feeling you could fly. Did I understand you correctly—fly?
— But only for a short while.
— How long, roughly?
— As long as I could keep moving my elbows.

Like wings. But that is very tiring. Even so, I nearly reached the ceiling in this room.

— That would be twenty-four feet.

— Actually, it isn't permitted, I knew that, but it was a sort of lust, also pride: you are the only person who can fly.

— And what happened next?

— A gliding flight.

— What do you mean by that?

— A curve, I managed besides to glide in a curve, but that was no longer in the courtroom; all at once a stretch of country, mountainous, a green reservoir beneath me, I was afraid my gliding flight wouldn't carry me to the bank—and the bank was perpendicular, a rocky cliff, absolutely perpendicular.

— And then you woke up, Herr Schaad?

— No.

— So what did happen?

— I was sitting here again. . . .

The bailiff has conducted sixty-one witnesses, male and female, into the chamber and shown them where to sit; some of them I knew only fleetingly.

— Major Zogg, you are the victim's father. . . .

There are some witnesses who look only at the judges, then at the prosecutor or defense attorney, never at the accused, though once they might have been called relatives.

— When did you last see your daughter?
— When Rosalinde was still married.
— So you were never inside her last apartment?
— Never.
— Did you know how your daughter was earning her living?
— You mean, after the divorce?
— Or did you have no idea?
— One has an idea what a doctor earns, and I assumed Rosalinde was being taken care of. According to her station, that is.
— So that as long as she lived she would not have to support herself. . . .
— Yes, that's what I mean: according to her station.
— Another question, Major Zogg.
— A letter written to my wife by the accused, informing her of the divorce—unfortunately, I no longer have it—sounded thoroughly reassuring.
— In what sense?
— He and Rosalinde wished to remain friends and so on.

The next witness is a child:

— Your name is Vreneli?
— Yes.

— You know Herr Schaad, sitting over there?
— No...
— You've never seen him before?
— Yes.
— You must only tell us what you know, Vre-
  neli. . . .

The girl nods.

— You know that Frau Rosalinde later died, but
  you saw her at the window. That's what you
  said. Can you remember when that was? I
  mean, what time of day? Was it still completely
  light outside?
— Yes.
— And she waved to you, as always?

The girl is silent.

— You don't know any longer. . . .

The girl nods.

— She came to the window?
— Yes.
— And what did she do then?
— I don't know.
— Was the window open?
— Yes.
— Did she shut the window?

— Yes.
— And then she drew the curtains?

The defense attorney is making notes.

— Vreneli, can you remember how Frau Rosalinde was dressed before she drew the curtains? Was she wearing her white dressing gown or her leather overcoat?

The girl is silent.

— You don't know any longer. . . .

The girl shrugs her shoulders.

— Did you see whether there was anyone else in her apartment? A man, maybe? A young man, an old man? Someone like Herr Schaad . . . ?

The girl shrugs her shoulders.

— Did you hear any screams?

The girl is silent.

— You don't know any longer. .
— No.
— Well, it was a long time ago.

I do not know whether here in Switzerland one needs a license to buy a revolver. The shop is closed on Sundays. One of the shotguns hanging in the small window might do it as well. The proprietor, since he is not in his shop on Sundays, could not be called as a witness. I do not believe that anyone else saw me in front of the shop window.

— That was this morning?
— Yes.
— And not a soul in the streets?
— It was rather early.
— When, approximately?
— Between seven and eight.
— What were you doing in town at this time, Herr Doktor Schaad, between seven and eight on Sunday morning, while Zurich was still asleep?
— I went for a walk. . . .

Alcohol does help sometimes. . . . I pace the room, glass in my right hand, and take the opportunity that only alcohol provides: I make a different final statement.

— I am not innocent . . .
— The truth and nothing but your truth . . .
— The shorter the better, my defense attorney says . . .
— I request the photograph of the naked corpse . . .

— I should like to thank, above all, the bailiff . . .
— Did any of you know this woman?
— I did not know her . . .
— I do not envy the jury, I freely admit; faced with this photograph, I share their solemn indifference . . .
— The shorter the better!
— Not since I was fourteen have I had the feeling of being innocent, that is true, though on the other hand I cannot say where I was that Saturday afternoon . . .
— That cannot be deduced from the photograph . . .
— I can speak as long as I wish . . .
— We no longer need the photograph . . .
— I come to the point . . .
— All the things you have discovered in my life story, Herr Prosecutor, I must congratulate you, you have worked hard . . .
— I should also like to thank the press . . .
— As for the motive . . .
— I also thank the forensic department for the black strip covering the corpse's vagina in the photograph you have seen several times; any teen-age boy can imagine that for himself . . .
— What is guilt?
— Only I did not do it . . .
— Or have I already said that?
— The circumstantial evidence gathered together by the prosecution cannot be dismissed out of

hand, that I admit; frankly, I'm shaken by it, and I thank my defense attorney for refusing to be shaken . . .
— Unfortunately, I am a little drunk at the moment . . .
— The witnesses are duty-bound to tell the truth and nothing but the truth . . .
— I wish to see the photograph once more . . .
— Thank you!
— I no longer need the photograph . . .
— I was lucky . . .
— Are you even listening?
— Ten years' penal servitude . . .
— And nothing but the truth . . .
— I also wish to thank the presiding judge for being so patient with my wives . . .

As soon as I am sober again, next morning at the latest, when I sit in my consulting room, hands clasped behind my neck and my feet on the desk, it continues:

— You were no longer relying on guesswork, you knew what trade she was engaged in, you say, and you felt at ease in her apartment, you were friends. . . .
— Yes.
— And what did you talk about?
— All kinds of topics.

— Did Rosalinde Z. tell you about her professional activities?

— Never.

— But you advised her on tax matters.

— She was so helpless. Like all my wives. And
that's my fault, I know. In my married life it
was always I who took care of such things, pref-
erably in secret, and when we were no longer
married, they were at a loss.

— So you knew what her income was?

— Not exactly, no, I just told her what expenses
could be deducted from her income, and these,
as I knew from our marriage, were considerable
sums: her clothes, her car, the hairdresser, etc.,
also theater tickets, I thought, and why not
books, records, etc.; there are many customers
who expect not just drinks but also an ambience of culture. She wasn't a streetwalker. And,
obviously, there were visitors who knew nothing of her profession, consequently had nothing to pay, but supplied the ambience and had
to be entertained for that purpose, as during
the time we were married.

— One last question, Herr Schaad.

— We were friends.

— How did that come about? I mean, what cured
you at last of your pathological jealousy?

— Video.

— I don't understand. . . .

— You don't know what video is?

— Of course I know.

— This was not done surreptitiously; it was her idea that I should once sit in the next room—without smoking!—and watch on the screen how she did it with other men, and was doing it at the very moment I was watching. I had inhibitions at first, but Rosalinde wished it. In order to cure me. It was a significant experience. I watched three of her customers on that occasion, and it was of course different each time, but on the other hand not all that different.

— Why was that a significant experience?

— Though the screen is quite small, I could distinctly see that as a rule sexual intercourse meant almost nothing to her. At best, she told me, she found coitus amusing. Even when her partner managed to transport her into ecstasies, that had nothing to do with personal sympathy. I don't know whether the second man noticed that. He didn't know that another had been there before him, and he had inherited her in a state of excitement that he found flattering. He took it personally. . . . Later we had dinner at the Kronenhalle, we talked of other things, and I had no feeling of being deceived. Actually, I could have known this long ago. Even during the time of our marriage. For Rosalinde bed was not a very personal sphere.

As I sit in my consulting room, hands clasped behind my head, looking out of the window (backyard
with five birch trees and a children's playground) or
staring at the green wall-to-wall carpeting, the brass
plate is still attached to the front door:

FELIX SCHAAD, M.D.
SPECIALIST IN INTERNAL MEDICINE
CONSULTATIONS BY APPOINTMENT

The Yugoslavian girl now hardly dares knock at the
door when she doesn't know what to do next. She is
probably reading or studying German. When my
arms begin to ache, I remove my hands from the
back of my neck and cut my fingernails.

— Does anybody else have a question?

The things a prosecutor manages to discover.

— "At the soccer match yesterday, I must admit, I
thought only of you, two teams as your bed-
fellows, eleven in white jerseys and eleven in
red jerseys, plus the bald referee and the two
linesmen, that makes twenty-five men exactly.
As you said. I could not stop thinking of it.
You are thirty-one, after all. How many men
had already slept with you was a question I
shouldn't have asked, yet you answered it so
honestly. Forgive my asking! But I took into

account on the soccer field something you also told me, that there were two you would prefer to forget, and so I eliminated the two linesmen, the rest was enough, you with two complete teams, plus the substitutes on the bench and one man warming up on the touchline, it was enough to drive me mad, and in the evening I see you under the shower—"

Three months after my acquittal (in the meantime I have sold my practice), the prosecutor is still at it:

— Nevertheless, letters like that, whether or not they were sent, reveal to us a pathological state of jealousy and paranoid tendencies which in no way preclude an unpremeditated act, a deed that the doer, of course, immediately sup-presses from his consciousness by recalling, for instance, how he fed seagulls or swans. . . .

Zurich is not a large city, it is inevitable that sooner or later, out in the streets, one should catch sight of somebody who appeared as a witness:

— I assume, Herr Stocker, that you always phoned beforehand and made an appointment, so that when the bell rang, Rosalinde Z. would usually know who was at the door.
— Of course.

— Did you ever find that the door to her apart-
ment was in fact unlocked, so that anybody
could simply turn the handle and enter?
— No.
— You never experienced that. . . .
— Never.
— Did you ever turn the handle without ringing
the bell?
— I do not do things like that.
— I assume, Herr Stocker, that on such visits you
occasionally made use of the bathroom. If so,
did you ever see a tie, a tie belonging to another
visitor?
— Yes, but not in the bathroom.
— Where, then?
— In the hall.
— Do you remember the color of that tie?
— I knew, of course, that I was not the only visitor
there, and consequently this tie was no affair of
mine. But I did notice it, that I admit. It was in
December. I even made a remark about it, I
believe, a little joke, and next time the tie was
no longer hanging in the guest closet.
— Then where was it?
— I don't know.
— Did you know whose tie it was?
— One doesn't ask such things, Herr Prosecutor.

When you happen to meet somebody in the street
whom you know only from the courtroom, who

should give the first nod, the acquitted or the witness?

— When did you visit Rosalinde Z. for the last time?
— In January.
— According to Rosalinde Z's appointment book, it was the sixth of February, and that would also tally with the date on your last Eurocheck, Herr Stocker.
— I don't have my appointment book with me.
— Another question, Herr Stocker.
— As for the check, I think you have the wrong idea. Rosalinde was not a prostitute or a street-walker, as you appear to imagine, Herr Prosecutor.
— What was she, then?
— Sometimes we only talked.
— And for that you gave her a check for this amount. . . .
— Naturally I asked myself how Rosalinde could pay for all these things, the comfortable apartment and everything, the smoked salmon and champagne, one knows what all that costs, and all the books lying on her bed.
— What sort of books were they?
— I am not much of an intellectual.
— You considered Rosalinde intellectual?
— Yes, I would definitely say so.

— About the books lying on the bed, Herr Stocker, did you have the impression that Rosalinde Z. read such books, or did they simply form part of the ambience?
— I don't understand the question. . . .
— Why were the books lying on the bed?
— I wondered about that too.
— And what did you talk about, Herr Stocker?
— People, and things like that.
— Herr Doktor Schaad, for example?
— No.
— Not a word?
— I knew there was a Herr Doktor Schaad.

There are also uninformative witnesses:

— Did Rosalinde Z. say she was Hungarian, or did you just assume that, Herr Spitzer, because you didn't expect so much charm in a woman with a Valaisan father and a mother from Appenzell?
— I am not prejudiced in that way.
— Have you known any real Hungarian women?
— Not really.
— Another question, Herr Spitzer: when you used the bathroom, did you ever notice a tie, another man's tie?
— No.
— Nor in the hall?
— No.

— Did you know about Herr Doktor Schaad?
— I thought his name was Zogg.

Nothing remains but billiards. I have also tried the movies, of course, but I rarely stay to the end, I cannot take scenes of violence—

— So you would also say that the accused is a person who would not hurt a fly?

Thirteen weeks after my acquittal, I now barely pay attention when I see the prosecutor indolently raising his hand to indicate that he has another question for the witness; he must wait until I have hit my ball, and if it is a winner, he must wait until I have walked around the table and, after calm consideration of the position (unfortunately, it can again only be done with a screw shot), have once more hit the ball:

— So, when your sister was married to Felix Schaad, you often saw her with eyes red from weeping?
— Yes.
— Herr Zogg, is it correct to say that Rosalinde was a gentle and tolerant person, the type of woman who would put up with virtually anything from a man she loved?
— She could be tolerant. . . .

— When you saw her red eyes, Herr Zogg, did you never have the suspicion that Rosalinde, your sister, might have been ill-treated by the accused, physically or mentally?

The witness reflects.

— Did Rosalinde never mention that Herr Doktor Schaad was jealous to a pathological degree, that he could hardly bear to see her dancing with another man, and that he made scenes when he did not know where she was for just one evening?
— My sister was always very discreet.

One should not leave notes lying around—someday one will be subjected to a false arrest and the prosecutor will read out:

— "She is a jellyfish, a jellyfish, even when for once she is not lying, and one cannot strangle a jellyfish."

Witnesses for the defense do not have an easy time:

— Herr Schaad saved my life.
— In what way?
— Not as a doctor ... I saw him feeding swans, and I went up and spoke to him, though I didn't

know him. I was still an apprentice at that time. It was Saturday, I know that, because afterward we had the general meeting.

— Was it raining?

— No.

— Or snowing?

— No.

— Then it wasn't the eighth of February.

— I didn't say it was. . . .

— You know, Herr Rossi, that perjury carries a prison sentence—in aggravated cases, up to five years' penal servitude, and this would be an aggravated case, Herr Rossi: it concerns an alibi for the accused.

— I am just telling the truth.

— Then how did Herr Schaad save your life?

— I can only say it wasn't what I expected when I blabbed to this stranger. You know what you get when you talk to older people! He was the first one who wasn't patronizing.

— Did Herr Schaad introduce himself to you?

— He just listened.

— And in that way saved your life . . .

— Yes.

— By feeding swans . . .

— In a way.

— Herr Rossi, this is a serious matter.

— He realized that; suddenly he asked how I meant to take my life. And I hadn't said a single

word about myself. Actually, I was clowning
around. Why I was thinking of killing myself at
that time I can't remember now. Herr Schaad
was quite matter-of-fact. Didn't preach. Just
sort of technical.
— Regarding suicide?
— Yes.
— So what did he tell you?
— I wish I knew. . . .
— And that, Herr Rossi, that was the conversation at the lake which, according to you, saved
your life when you were still an apprentice?
— Herr Schaad himself maybe doesn't know it.

Sometimes even the accused hears something new
to him.

— You are a commercial artist?
— Designer.
— And you knew the accused?
— I still know him.
— You were friends at the time Rosalinde, then
your wife, was having a clandestine affair with
Herr Doktor Schaad in Zurich.
— Yes.
— But you were friends. . . .
— We took walks together.
— Is it correct, Herr Schwander, that during one
of these walking tours, when the accused tried

to talk to you about your marriage, you simply refused to listen? This, according to Herr Schaad, was on the Albis, near Zurich, and you sat in a restaurant for three hours, but you simply refused to listen, Herr Schwander, to the story of his affair with Rosalinde. Is that correct?

— I remember. . . .

— Why did you refuse to listen?

— I knew about another affair Rosalinde was having at that time, and I had the impression that Felix knew nothing about it, and I didn't wish to talk about my marriage, that's a fact.

The prosecutor has discovered another note revealing my pathological conditions:

— "For example, I watch her peeling asparagus, we talk about nothing in particular, then suddenly I find myself counting the stiff peeled stalks of asparagus on the kitchen table, twenty-four; I say nothing, of course, but I think to myself: There's one missing."

How many panels are there in the courtroom ceiling? I estimate thirty-six. The room is an oblong. That would mean—four by nine? I try a second estimate: it turns out to be forty-five. Squares or rhomboids? I decide on squares. And the beams are painted in some way, that I know, whereas the pan-

els are whitewashed. Or is it the other way around?
In the center, an imposing chandelier. I know: when
the sun is shining outside, one scarcely notices it;
only on rainy days does one need its imposing light.
How many branches does this chandelier have? I
would maintain: they are brass. But I admit: I do not
know, although I sat there for at least a hundred
hours with folded arms, my eyes on the ceiling, as
wives gave testimony about their marriages.

— You are Frau Professor Jetzer?
— I am not a professor.
— Frau Jetzer, then . . .
— Thank you.
— First name?
— Helene Mathilde.
— Your maiden name was Knuchel?
— I am a housewife.
— You were the first wife of the accused, Frau
  Jetzer, and that was a long time ago. Of course,
  you do not need to make any depositions if you
  can no longer remember. . . .

It helps the accused when one can see that he is
touched, and when for once he is sitting there, not
with folded arms, but with openness and good will,
before the witness replies.

— You have understood my question, Frau Jetzer?
— We were both very young.

69

— Felix Schaad never struck you or threatened you with violence, he took the garbage downstairs on his way to work, on Sundays he washed the dishes, and so on. . . . What else do you remember, Frau Jetzer?

— We did not have much money.

— I am asking about particular events.

— Felix was an assistant physician.

— So you did not have much money. . . .

— Very little.

— And what else do you remember?

— We went walking a lot.

— Didn't you ever get the impression, Frau Jetzer, that Felix Schaad had a pathological tendency toward jealousy, even if, as a rule, he kept it under control? I mean, even when he had no cause for jealousy.

— He had no cause for it.

— You went walking a lot. . . .

— With a tent in summer.

— You both liked the outdoors. . . .

— In winter we went cross-country skiing.

— So what led to your divorce?

— I think we were both disappointed.

— For what reason?

— It was my first marriage, too.

— Later you married again, Frau Jetzer, you are the mother of three daughters; obviously it is not your fault if a marriage proves untenable.

— I, too, have grown more mature since then. . . .

One overestimates the memories of people who read the popular press. I can pass with impunity a booth in which only a few weeks ago my portrait was prominently displayed: NO ALIBI FOR SCHAAD / BLUEBEARD IN COURT / DOCTOR'S SEVEN MARRIAGES. And I am still wearing the suit I wore in court. Even when I go to buy new glasses, and the optician, having just written down my name, has to peer right into his patient's eyes in order to measure the distance between the pupils, I have no sense of being recognized.

— What does the cross mean to you, Herr Schaad?

One is also questioned about dreams:

— And how large was this cross?
— Small. About the size of a traffic warning triangle. That's why I wanted to place it on the road. As a warning sign. But suddenly it got too big, almost as big as myself. The size of a cross on a grave.
— And where did you get this cross?
— No idea.
— If it was as small as a warning triangle, Herr Schaad, might you not have found it in the trunk of your car when you were looking for the actual warning triangle?
— That's possible. . . .
— And how did it get into the trunk?

— No idea . . .

— So you wished, you say, to put this warning sign on the road, and when the passers-by noticed that it was a wrought-iron memorial cross, they stopped and stared.

— There was suddenly a whole crowd.

— Can you describe this cross more precisely?

— It was rather heavy.

— Can you go into more detail?

— I think it was rusty.

— You wished to stick it in the asphalt?

— Yes.

— As a warning sign?

— I believe so.

— Did the onlookers say anything?

— I heard nothing. No. In any case, I was expecting to be arrested.

— Why?

— Because the cross did not belong to me.

— You were aware of that, Herr Schaad?

— One man asked where I had got it from, this cross, but he wasn't a policeman. More like a connoisseur. He showed the sort of interest an antique dealer might have, but he didn't ask the price.

— And then?

— I felt ashamed.

— Do you know why you felt ashamed?

— Because it just couldn't be done, and I kept on and on trying to ram the cross into the asphalt,

as everybody could see, but it just couldn't be
done. . . .
— That woke you up?
— I was covered with sweat. . . . All I know is that
it had suddenly turned into a Mafia, or so it
seemed to me, and I wasn't at all surprised;
when I went to put the cross back in the trunk,
my car had been stolen. Under the very noses
of witnesses! But they hadn't noticed a thing, or
they were no longer there. . . .

Traveling abroad is no help at all, Japan, for instance, where nobody knows about the trial and nobody has listened to the witnesses; then I sit, hands
clasping my left or my right knee, on a bench in the
Imperial Gardens in Kyoto and hear the psychiatrist's expert testimony:

— A paranoid element is undeniably present, a
fairly common symptom in alcoholics. It finds
an outlet, as we have seen, predominantly in
letters which are frequently never sent, although this shows that the accused as a rule has
become aware, after only a few hours, of the
extent to which he has allowed himself to be
led astray by surmises. I initially made reference
to his pent-up emotionality. To sum up: there
is no evidence of diminished responsibility in
the accused. . . .

Rock gardens, etc., the pearl-diving girls of wherever, it is all familiar, no matter whether one was
ever in Japan. This is not enough for an alibi. Even if
I relate how the Japanese masseuse went walking
down my spine on her little heels, it does not prove I
was in Japan; that, too, I could have read somewhere.

— As regards the Japanese rock gardens which
    you claim to have visited that Sunday, Herr
    Doktor Schaad, and the little pearl-diving girls
    of Mikimoto—that's the name of the place—
    you learned about that from one of the maga-
    zines lying in your waiting room. You realize
    that, Herr Doktor Schaad?

A stopover in Hong Kong is also of little help. Two
nights in a Chinese brothel. Even during a boat trip
around the harbor, I recall the questions asked by
members of the jury:

— I, too, have read all the letters placed before the
    court, and I should like to ask Herr Doktor
    Schaad whether a woman doesn't have the
    right to burn love letters.
— Well, yes, of course . . .
— Then why did you make copies?

— You have been divorced six times, Herr Doktor

Schaad, but why did your marriages keep getting shorter?

— Life is getting shorter.
— Don't you have the impression, Herr Doktor
Schaad, that the fault may be yours? So why do
you keep on marrying?

— I should like to ask the accused whether he
thinks he has ever understood a woman. For
this doesn't seem to me to be the case, Herr
Doktor: you are always puzzling about women,
and if a woman doesn't conform to your mas-
culine interpretation, what then?

— Concerning the flowers that were found with
the body, the murder happened in February,
didn't it, so they could only be hothouse lilies,
that's obvious, and as far as the lilies are concerned, well, we've seen them in the photograph, and as a gardener I'd just like to ask one
question: does the court know how long hothouse lilies last? As an expert, I believe only the
murderer could have brought these lilies; otherwise they wouldn't be as fresh as the ones
we've seen in the photograph. . . . That's not a
question, just an observation.

Also unforgettable is a friend:

— You conversed with the accused mainly about

astronomy, so we have been told, Herr Neuenburger, and you also enjoy drinking wine with
him, a vintage Bordeaux, although the accused,
you assure us, doesn't know anything about astronomy, or so you have told us.

— That's because he refuses to think.

— Herr Neuenburger . . .

— Otherwise he's a good guy.

— Did you know Rosalinde Z.?

— I've never met a doctor who could think. I've
got a doctor of my own who is surprised I'm
still alive, and grateful to me because I am. A
doctor who has never killed anybody is just
lucky. . . .

— To come back to my question . . .

— Schaad was just unlucky.

— How did he speak about Rosalinde?

— At the time I was into Einstein. . . .

— You mean, Schaad couldn't get a word in edge-
wise?

— It's difficult, of course, to talk about Einstein
when the other person has no conception of
mathematics, but luckily I've got two dogs, and
all you have to do to change the subject is pat
your thigh and they're there; dog stories are
always good fun. . . . Schaad just has no sense of
humor. . . . I wouldn't like to be his wife, either. . . . Listen, I've been married twenty-four
years, and that's where humor comes in, you

can't carry it off without a sense of humor; my
wife too almost became an actress. . . .
— When did you last see Rosalinde?
— He introduced me to all the women he married,
and each time called on God to curse him if he
ever deceived her.
— What do you mean by that?
— It's grotesque, isn't it?

The witness chuckles.

— Herr Neuenburger . . .
— I feel sorry for Schaad.
— You have called Rosalinde Z. a stupid cow, but
on the other hand you once gave her a drawing
with a dedication. . . .
— Then I must have been thinking of one of the
others.
— But we are concerned with Rosalinde Z.
— I was never interested in my friend's marriages,
and I believe he appreciated that. And I myself
never talk about my marriage. In matters of sex,
my mind gives out.
— A final question, Herr Neuenburger.
— A doctor who is not aware of the revolution
going on in biochemistry, it's grotesque, and I'd
much prefer a walk with my two dogs. . . .
— To return to the accused . . .
— My dogs always get on his nerves.

— In what way is Herr Schaad a good guy?

— After all, we've been friends for at least thirty years, though we've got nothing to say to each other. But I enjoy drinking my wine with him. I myself don't need friends. I can think for myself.

— You talked about Einstein. . . .

— I keep coming back to Einstein, his thinking has a significance that is not fully appreciated even today. Philosophically, that is. I am philosophical myself; my wife is more the musical type.

— That was not my question.

— It's his falsehoods that bother me; then there's no choice but to talk about Einstein; once Schaad starts on the subject of himself, well, absolutely none of it rings true. . . .

— Can you cite an example?

— I don't want to say anything derogatory about him.

— Do you remember what your friend the accused said when he managed to get a word in?

— I don't recall. . . .

— As a witness, Herr Neuenburger, you have a duty to tell the truth and nothing but the truth; you know, don't you, that perjury carries a prison sentence. . . .

— And then Schaad is so hypersensitive.

— When he hears what you have been saying behind his back . . .

— Then he doesn't phone me for a whole year.
— But you call him?
— That's what he waits for, I believe. .... And by then Schaad has got married again, and I didn't even know he'd divorced this Rosemarie!

The witness chuckles to himself.

— One final question, Herr Neuenburger ...

Journeys end in homecomings.
(Zurich-Kloten airport)
The cab driver, Hungarian and friendly, knows the route he has to take—that is, via the Kreuzplatz. My witness there, the garage owner, is just filling a tank.

— So you got the impression he was drunk?
— Well, he didn't remember he'd already been there in the morning, or what I had told him in the morning about his clutch.
— You had known him as a customer before?
— For years.
— So when did he bring his Volvo in?
— In the morning, I'm sure about that, and if the doctor hadn't been an old customer, I wouldn't have promised he'd be able to drive into the country that same day. We've only got one mechanic working on Saturdays.
— When did Herr Schaad return?
— Shortly after noon.

— Shortly after noon . . .

— That's when I told him his clutch wouldn't last much longer. It was just about worn out. It's a long job changing a clutch, you know.

— So his car was not ready at noon. . . .

— Afraid not.

— So he could not drive into the country. . . .

— The doctor was disappointed, but that was all I could do for him that Saturday, and the doctor immediately understood; I told him I'd have another try at tightening the clutch.

— When did Herr Schaad return?

— Shortly before six. As arranged.

— And his car was working?

— In a manner of speaking.

— When the accused came to the garage shortly before six, was he still wearing a tie, as at noon?

— In a manner of speaking.

— Yes or no?

— Well, it hung a bit crooked, his tie, and rather loose, like it does when you've been drinking too much, and that's why I wouldn't hand the car over, it would have cost him his driver's license at the very least. You could smell it on him. What good is a doctor without a driver's license?

— That was not my question, Herr Lüscher.

— You could smell it on him.

— I asked you whether or not the accused, when

you saw him shortly before six on that Saturday, was wearing a tie.

— I've told you already.

The clutch is still the same today.

— Herr Schaad, why do you keep shaking your
head?

I am waiting to this day for my state-appointed defense attorney, after three weeks spent extracting
exonerating statements from wives, to make known
to the nine jury members something that is also part
of the truth:

— Let me remind you of his four years' participa-
tion in the district council, his expert advice on
hospital construction, not to mention his personal contribution to the care and accommoda-
tion of Czech refugees, his public fight against
the pollution of our lakes, his daily work as a
highly respected practicing physician; I remind
you, further, of his selfless contributions in
Biafra some years ago, where he worked for
three months as a doctor, and his numerous
lectures on family planning, not to mention his
concern with drug addiction among our young
people, his painstaking study of acupuncture
and, not least, his successes with acupuncture.

After all, a life story does not consist solely of marriages! Last but not least, let me remind you of his interest in music, for example. . . .

The prosecutor has unearthed another note:

— "When there is a frequent absence of erections, as is the case at present, every woman seems tempted to doubt all a man's other capabilities. No day without a few petty admonitions. And it is true, I do make one mistake after another: on social occasions, behind the wheel of my car, in the garden, etc., but not, I hope, in the hospital."

Help comes on one occasion from the gardener on the jury:

— I should like to ask the accused, I mean, regarding this matter and to keep to the point, this Rosalinde Z. wasn't, after all, a frustrated woman, it seems to me, at the time she was murdered, so why should she nag Herr Doktor Schaad, who looked after her tax matters, into becoming a murderer? That doesn't make sense to me.

Sometimes I stay in the bathtub after the water has drained out and only the faucet is dripping. I lie with my eyes closed and hear:

— We did have a Spanish maid, and sometimes Felix would do the cooking, if he was in the mood. Please don't think I'm complaining. After all, he knew I wasn't his servant.
— He knew that. . . .
— Felix was always very generous.
— But you felt dependent on him, economically speaking. . . .
— I can't deny that.

This could be the fair-haired Andrea.

— I also play the violin, for instance.
— But you never got around to playing. . . .
— That may also be my fault.
— What is your fault, Frau Schaad?
— I demand a great deal of myself.
— And Felix Schaad did not understand that?
— I often went to Eranos meetings.
— What are they?
— A university would have been better for me, he thought, some sort of studies with seminars and examinations, but exactly what kind of studies he didn't know, either.
— I see. . . .
— But that doesn't mean I was just a housewife.
— Quite right.
— I married Schaad because I loved him.
— What job did you have before your marriage?
— I had to earn a living, after all.

— You were a substitute teacher?
— That is correct.
— And what do you do now?
— I no longer have any faith in this country's educational system.
— And you can live on that, Frau Doktor Schaad?

I shampoo my hair.

— So you, too, Frau Doktor Schaad, would say that the accused is a person who would not hurt a fly.
— I wouldn't put it like that.
— How would you put it?
— When he's beside himself, I mean, when he loses his head, or how I shall I put it, he is capable of ripping his shirt, I've seen that more than once, or he picks up some object and smashes it in front of me.
— What sort of object?
— Whatever is around . . .
— Such as?
— If he couldn't do it in front of me, I think he wouldn't do it at all. His glasses, for instance, or he smashes his pipe in front of me, his very best one, to punish me.
— What for?
— That's exactly what drives him so crazy: I never know what he's trying to punish me for. All I see is him smashing his expensive pipes, one

after another, because I can't understand why
he's angry with me. He threw his watch out of
the window once.
— Objects, in other words, that belong to him . . .
— That's what I mean when I say *introverted*.
— He doesn't hit out at other people, then?
— I've never seen him do that.
— You have never seen him do that. . . .
— He'd sooner strangle himself.

That is Gisel.
(She, too, has put on weight.)
I shampoo my hair.

— And when he had been drinking, Frau Schaad,
something you, too, have witnessed, he would
pace the room talking.
— Oh, yes.
— You, too, have witnessed that. . . .
— I used to let him talk.
— Without contradicting him?
— That's what he was waiting for.
— And then you would go off to bed?
— It was midnight.
— And what did he do?
— Made me feel sorry for him.

That is Corinne.
(Or Andrea?)
I rinse my hair.

— Did you know, Frau Doktor, that Felix Schaad, while married to you, kept a sort of secret diary?

The witness is silent.

— You did not know that.
— I suspected it.
— Why?
— When things got tense between us, I mean, when Felix acted as though he'd had enough, something, I suppose, that happens in any marriage, well, we used to have a dog and he'd go for a walk in the woods with the dog, but when our dog got run over we didn't want another one, and so, when things got tense, Felix would go to his study instead of to the woods, and it was then I suspected he was maybe keeping a diary, because after an hour or so he seemed to have calmed down. I certainly noticed that. When he came out of his study he behaved as if there was nothing more to be said.
— Since he had put his views down on paper.
— He was like another person.
— And it didn't hurt you that your husband, instead of saying what he thought in open argument, scribbled it all down in a notebook?
— I suspected he was doing that. . . .
— Didn't you ever read any of his notebooks?

— I knew where he hid them.
— And you weren't curious?
— Well, I had no way of knowing what he said to our dog when he took it walking in the woods, either.
— So you were not curious. . . .
— Sometimes I found those notebooks in his coat pocket, but, frankly, I didn't find what Felix scribbled in his notebooks very interesting.
— So you did snoop?
— No.
— Then how, Frau Doktor, do you happen to know what is contained in these notebooks? Incidentally, there are dozens of them.
— All I needed to do was wait.
— What do you mean by that?
— When things got tense again, Felix couldn't keep quiet about what he'd been thinking the last time or the time before that.
— And that didn't interest you?
— Frankly, no . . .

That is Lilian.
(The mother of my son)
I dry my hair.

— How long have you had a driver's license, Frau Doktor?
— I'd have to look that up.

— Approximately?

— Since I came of age, I believe.

— Have you ever been responsible for an accident, Frau Doktor? Not just superficial damage; I mean the sort of accident that would make Felix Schaad worry about you if you were alone at the wheel?

— I drive better than he does.

— Are you fully insured?

— Liability, I think.

— So you consider yourself a safe driver. Rightly so. After all, you never had a serious accident, Frau Schaad, either before your marriage or as Frau Doktor Schaad, when you drove a Morris.

— It was a Fiat.

— Later, yes, after the Morris.

— I am still driving the Fiat.

— Frau Doktor Schaad, do you remember a marital squabble in Milan? The accused, at that time your husband, wanted to let you drive home by yourself, in order to put an end to the squabble, while he would go by plane. Is that correct? Whereupon you are reported to have said: VERY WELL, THEN I'LL DRIVE INTO A TREE.

— Married people say all sorts of things.

— How did Herr Schaad respond to this?

The witness reflects.

— Did he say to you: THEN GO AHEAD AND DRIVE INTO A TREE—or did he call it blackmail?

— That wasn't in Milan at all.

— Where was it, Frau Schaad?

— In Piacenza, I think; I mean, I'm sure it was Piacenza, and he wanted to take a cab to Milan, but he didn't, and we drove over the Gotthard together.

— Who took the wheel on that occasion?

— I did.

— With regard to the tree, the accused asserts there are sentences he knows for certain he could never have uttered, such as the sentence THEN GO AHEAD AND DRIVE INTO A TREE—which is clearly the reason he became so angry when you later told his friends that Schaad had said to you: THEN GO AHEAD AND DRIVE INTO A TREE.

— They were my friends.

— But is it true, Frau Schaad, that you did say that, and that he threatened you with divorce if you did not retract this assertion and, what's more, in writing?

— And that's what I did.

— Then I have no further questions.

That is Andrea:

— But all the same he did say it.

There is no common memory.

— Can the witness stand down?

Once, the only time in three weeks, the old district judge, who cups his left ear as witnesses testify, asks a question:

— Do you know, Herr Doktor Schaad, what a car looks like, a FIAT, for instance, when it has been driven into a tree?
— No.
— Of course, it depends on the speed.
— I can see that.
— So you have never seen a car that, at the legally permitted speed of fifty miles an hour, has been driven into a tree?

They still have one more wife to examine.

— So you, Frau Doktor Schaad, are not divorced?
— No.
— You are married to Felix Schaad?
— Yes.
— Is that right?

We smile at each other.

— When you got married a year ago, Frau Doktor, I take it you knew about the past of the accused, including his six marriages—or did you first learn about it from this trial?
— Most of it I knew.

— And it did not alarm you?

— I have a past, too.

— Is it correct, Frau Schaad, that you occasionally addressed the accused as Chevalier Bluebeard?

— That is a term of endearment. . . .

— You think so?

— Felix is chivalrous.

— And what precisely made you think of Bluebeard?

— He once said he already had six wives in his cellar, and I am fully aware that his previous wives are living quite well.

— Except for Rosalinde Z.

The witness is silent.

— Did you know this Rosalinde Z.?

— He told me about her.

— What, for instance?

— What she thought of the new Pope.

— So you were aware that Herr Doktor Schaad paid regular visits to her, and that did not bother you at all?

— No.

— Is it right, Frau Schaad, that you and Herr Doktor Schaad see each other only rarely, that you take trips together but do not live with each other?

— That is right.

— You find that right. . . .
— I am hardly a teen-ager any longer, Herr Prosecutor, I am thirty-six years old, and I made up
my mind years ago that I should never again
live with a man.
— And Herr Schaad understands that?
— He is chivalrous.
— Nevertheless, I have one more question. If I
have read your letters correctly, Frau Schaad,
you stated from the very beginning that you
were not prepared to resist an occasional attrac-
tion to another man, and so on.
— I don't understand the question. . . .
— How did the accused react to that?
— If anything changes between us, my husband
can rest assured that I shall let him know.
— And Herr Doktor Schaad accepts that. . . .
— Anyway, one isn't always sure at the start, and
it usually turns out to be a mistake; after a cou-
ple of weeks it's not all that exciting with another man. I don't consider it necessary for
Felix to know every time.
— And he is aware of that. . . .

That is Jutta.
(At present in Kenya)
Witnesses are always more credible than the accused, for which reason the defense attorney prefers
to address himself to the witness:

— So you would call it a happy marriage. . . .

I looked it up in the library: the tale of the knight who killed his seven wives and concealed their corpses in the cellar was written by a Frenchman, Charles Perrault, in the seventeenth century.

— I hereby declare the proceedings closed. The jury will retire to consider the evidence. Verdict will be announced on Friday morning at eleven o'clock.

Reading newspapers helps for a little while.
The Pope will recover. . . .
Rosalinde stays dead.

— Do you often get asked by a visitor where a particular grave is located? I'm not talking now of Joyce's grave, but the grave of some family relation.
— Once in a while.
— You have never heard of the Schaad case?
— No.
— The acquitted maintains that he had to ask three times before you finally switched the lawn mower off in order to hear what the gentleman wanted.
— All the graves are marked.

— So you did not know the whereabouts of the grave he was looking for, and you went on mowing. Is that correct? And the gentleman watched you?

— For a while, yes, that's correct.

— How long?

— He watched as if he'd never seen a lawn mower before, and by then it had begun to rain; that was shortly before six, I think. And we close the cemetery at six.

— Did Herr Schaad know that?

— It's on the noticeboard at the entrance.

— While he was watching you mow, did the acquitted ask you any other questions, or didn't you hear him?

— He walked on.

— Is it correct, Herr Knapp, that the acquitted walked off initially in the opposite direction, although you had told him approximately where he might find the graves from February of last year?

— Maybe he didn't hear.

— Because of the lawn mower.

— Our lawn mowers are not all that loud.

— Can you show us on this plan where you were cutting the grass yesterday, Herr Knapp, when the acquitted inquired about the graves from February of last year?

— Here, yes, about here . . .

— So it's not far from the entrance gate?

— Where the lawn is, that's where.

— And that was shortly before six o'clock, you say, and the cemetery spreads out quite a bit, particularly when one walks off initially in the wrong direction. . . .

— Let's say a quarter to six.

— Is it possible, do you think, Herr Knapp, that the gentleman, having set off in the wrong direction, could have found the grave he was looking for in a quarter of an hour, before he was obliged to leave the cemetery?

— Hardly.

— You didn't see him again?

— Maybe it was earlier, after all: five-thirty, say. I can't cut grass up to six in any case. Maybe he left the cemetery while I was putting the mower in the shed. And then the mower has to be cleaned. And whether people find their graves or not, I mean the graves of their relatives, that's no business of mine anyway. I'm responsible for the grass and for putting the wreaths on the compost heap, and I finish work at six.

— One final question, Herr Knapp.

— Why should anyone want to spend the night in a cemetery?

— When the acquitted, as you have told us, walked on the grass, which is strictly prohibited, was he carrying flowers of any kind?

— I don't think so.

— Lilies, for example?

Then:

— When was this, Frau Hofer?
— Today.
— At what time?
— This morning. I was surprised, because I was the first visitor after they opened the gate, and that is always at nine, I'm sure of that, nine o'clock precisely.
— What surprised you?
— How the gentleman came to be there already.
— Did I understand you correctly, Frau Hofer? The grave you were tending is in the same row as Rosalinde Zogg's grave?
— Yes, unfortunately, it is.
— Did you know about the Schaad case?
— Luckily, my husband knows nothing about it.
— So you were surprised, Frau Hofer; and how did this gentleman behave when he saw you coming?
— He was standing in my way.
— How do you mean?
— I don't think he saw me or even heard me, though on these gravel paths you can hear every step. But he was just standing there. Usually I come from the right side, but I didn't wish to disturb the gentleman in his devotions.
— It was the first time you had seen him?
— It's a year since my husband died, and I visit the

cemetery once a week, but I've never seen anybody at that grave before. He was just standing
there with his hands in his pockets, that's all I
can tell you, and, yes, as I came up from the
other side, he suddenly took out a cigarette and
lit it and walked away.

— Did the gentleman look unshaven?
— I didn't look at him that closely.
— And the grave, Frau Hofer, the grave next to
your late husband's, I mean: did you notice
anything there?
— The pile of cigarette butts.
— What else?
— Well, it still has no tombstone, only the ever-
green provided by the cemetery, and the plate
with the number on it.
— No flowers?
— There were a few lilies lying there. . . .
— How fresh were these lilies?
— It's happened two or three times before, they
stay there a whole week, just a few lilies, till the
gardener collects them and throws them away.

Then:

— So you do not deny, Herr Schaad, that you
spent the night in the cemetery, against the
rules?
— No.

— What were you hoping to achieve?

— I didn't intend to do it. . . .

— You found the gate locked.

— That's right.

— Why didn't you ring the gatekeeper's bell? There must be a gatekeeper there when the cemetery is closed. And there is a telephone booth beside the gate. Why didn't you call the police?

— It didn't enter my mind. . . .

— So you remained in the cemetery, although it was raining; and what did you do all that time?

— It wasn't raining for long.

— Did I understand you correctly, Herr Doktor Schaad? This was your first visit to that grave?

— Yes.

— Although you had once been married to the victim . . . A year ago, when the funeral took place, you had not yet been arrested, Herr Doktor Schaad. The arrest came later. And you knew at the time when and where the funeral would take place. Why didn't you go to the funeral?

— I have already been asked that at the preliminary hearing.

— You were not out of town.

— No.

— You were in your consulting room when the victim was buried, treating patients who could easily have waited another two hours. Is that correct? You had to see, according to the files, a chronic migraine, a case of prostate trouble which you referred to the urologist, and a lady whom you were able to inform that some tests had proved satisfactory. Not emergency cases, therefore.

— That is correct.

— Yet you stayed away from the funeral.

— That is correct.

— Isn't that curious, Herr Schaad?

— Yes.

— According to the files, you said at the preliminary hearing that you dislike funerals, that you can't stand it when a Protestant parson tries to describe a deceased person whom he has never seen.

— That is what I said.

— As to your present visit to the cemetery: did you spend the whole night standing by her grave?

— No.

— What else did you do?

— Later I found a bench, and I must have gone to sleep for a while; it was only at daybreak that I went back to the grave, to see if the five lilies were still there.

— Did you bring those lilies?

— No.

— Then who did bring those lilies?
— I spent the whole night asking myself that.

The presiding judge interrupts with a question:

— You told the psychiatrist that Rosalinde Z. had never experienced sexual fulfillment. Not with her previous partners, either. How do you know that?
— She told me.
— And why did she tell you that?
— In the interests of truth . . .
— You are a physician, Herr Doktor Schaad, so I assume that you discussed openly and objectively what Rosalinde Z. understood by sexual fulfillment.
— I do not wish to say anything more about it.
— And when did she tell you this?
— After the divorce . . . Up to that moment I was convinced that the fault was mine. She was then in her early thirties. All I knew was that she feared her life would remain unfulfilled, and I did not wish to be the cause of that.
— And that was your reason for demanding a divorce?
— I loved her.
— That was the reason for divorce. . . .
— Right.

A telephone call from Neuenburger, saying he now has a vintage Bordeaux that tops everything. He means well, I know. He chuckles. Surely I couldn't have expected a trial by jury to produce anything but a farce? He chuckles so loudly that I have to remove the receiver some distance from my ear.

— So you cannot say, Herr Schaad, who the woman was who, you claim, placed the three pills in your hand?
— No.
— She was trying to help you?
— In a way.
— You had a revolver in your hand, you say, rather a small one. Where you got it from you don't even know. And you can't even specify the make. All you knew was that it was loaded, and the safety catch was off.
— That I did know.
— All the same, it didn't go off?
— I tried three times.
— And you thought you were alone?
— I was alone.
— But where all this happened you don't know, either. Whether in the woods or in your consulting room. So you placed the revolver against your right temple, Herr Doktor Schaad, and you fully intended to shoot yourself. . . .
— What else?

— Did you have any particular reason for it?

— I knew what I was doing.

— And this woman who was all of a sudden there watching as the revolver failed to go off: you cannot tell us the color of her hair?

— No.

— Nevertheless, you recognized this woman?

— She looked very familiar to me, oh, yes. . . .

— So it was not just any person watching as the ridiculous revolver failed to go off and suddenly handing over three pills, with the instruction that one would be enough for your purpose? It was someone with whom you were involved?

— Oh, yes . . .

— And she smiled.

— She really wanted to help.

— What happened then?

— I could feel I was being observed; first there was just a small group of people, obviously her new friends, but suddenly there were others there as well, watching me be too cowardly to swallow those three pills that would do the trick.

The accused has to rise when the verdict is announced; the three judges and the nine jurors remain seated, all carefully maintaining expressions that will not betray to the court which of them opted for guilty and which for not guilty during the seven hours of deliberation; prosecutor and defense attorney are no longer facing the accused, but sit on their chairs to the right and to the left, both with their eyes fixed calmly on the ceiling; the courtroom is crowded, the prosecutor's plea already known: ten years' penal servitude, minus the time spent in detention on remand. And outside the sun is shining; that makes the courtroom look so bright. The accused is on his feet; only his hands reveal that a judicial error is not unimaginable to him. And then, after he has heard the verdict, he rests his hands on the little table, his chin begins to wobble, he weeps—for joy, apparently—with lowered head.

ACCORDING TO THE EVIDENCE THE COURT FINDS:

1) The accused, Felix Theodor Schaad, M.D., is not guilty of the crime of which he stands accused and is acquitted.

2) The costs of the preliminary and final court hearings are chargeable to the state.

3) For the detention on remand for a period of 291 days and the inconvenience suffered by process of law the accused is granted a sum of 178,000 francs in compensation.

4) For notification to the office of the Public Prosecutor, to the accused, to the aggrieved parties, and to the psychiatric expert, Professor Doktor Herbert Vetter.

5) Appeals against this verdict are admissible as legal measure of redress by pleas of nullity to the cantonal and federal authorities; both must be submitted within ten days to the President of the Court of Assizes.

Because of insufficient evidence—
Where did I hear that?
It is not mentioned in the verdict.

THE COURT FURTHER ANNOUNCES:

1) The instruments used in the course of the criminal act and the replica of the apartment on the Hornstrasse are to be delivered to the cantonal police authority in Zurich for use at its discretion.

2) The documents confiscated from the residence and office of the accused, viz. letters, photographs, diaries, etc., will be delivered to the accused after legal confirmation of the findings for disposal at his own discretion.

Suicide following an acquittal because of insufficient evidence is out of the question; it would be interpreted as a belated confession.
What has to be done:
a new tax statement
(loss of earnings through detention on remand)
dental hygiene
etc.

— You are Herr Schaad?
— Yes.
— First name Hermann.
— Yes.
— You are the father of the acquitted?

The judicial warning that perjury carries a prison sentence—in aggravated cases, up to five years' penal servitude—does not apply to the interrogation of the dead:

— Do you recall the rabbit? Felix was nine years old, and you gave him a rabbit. Is that correct? A gray rabbit . . .

Documents such as letters, photographs, diaries, etc., have to be collected by me personally from the cantonal police headquarters in Zurich; my tie remains in the same place, for use at their discretion.

— Your son, Herr Schaad, has been acquitted. . . .

What helps is walking.
(Albis)
My father was a teacher:

— Do you know what *Nagelfluh* is?
— *Nagelfluh* is a rock.
— Is that right?
— This is *Nagelfluh*, you can see that by the many small stones in it, and what's typical of those is that they're so round, these stones, like pebbles in a stream, which shows that they've come a long way and have been ground down in the process; the whole of the Albis consists in part of *Nagelfluh*.
— And what is *Nagelfluh*?
— Moraine.
— That is correct.
— And all these stones once fell onto the glaciers from the highest peaks, when the glaciers were there, then they were rolled about in glacial meltwater, that's why they're so round. Then the glaciers disappeared, but before that they'd pressed this gravel together over millions of years, which is why *Nagelfluh* is as hard as rock, but it isn't genuine rock, it's *Nagelfluh*.
— And what else do you know?
— *Nagelfluh* is a typical feature of our country.

— And what else is there?
— Sandstone and limestone.
— And what else?
— Slate.
— I am thinking of something different now.
— But there is slate, too. . . .
— Don't you know what I am thinking of?
— Glaciers once covered our whole country, and that's why there are glacial striations on the rocks and *Nagelfluh*, which is useful for gravel pits.
— And what else?
— Lakes . . .
— We're talking about rocks, Felix.
— I don't know. . . .
— What do we see here in the woods?
— That is an erratic block.
— Right!
— You can find those, too, but they're rare.
— And what is an erratic block?
— An erratic block is a genuine rock, but it comes from somewhere else, and it also has something to do with these glaciers, which later disappeared, and the erratic block was left over when the Ice Age ended, because the glacier didn't carry it any farther; that is an erratic block, for instance, a slate.
— Is that slate?
— No.

— What is it, then?
— An erratic block.
— Is it granite?
— No.
— What is granite?
— Quartz, feldspar, and mica.
— That is correct.

A letter from Kenya:
SEE YOU SOON! JUTTA
I start emptying the ashtrays.

— So you call it by and large a happy marriage,
Frau Schaad, if I understand you correctly, an
open marriage, you have your personal free-
dom and feel in no way threatened by Felix
Schaad, your husband. . . .
— That is right.
— You describe him as thoroughly chivalrous. . . .

What again is no help: alcohol.

— You were the mother of Felix Schaad?
— Yes, indeed.
— You had a long life, Frau Schaad, nearly eighty
years. But perhaps you recall a few incidents
from Felix's school years. . . .
— Yes, indeed.
— The prosecutor will question you first. . . .

Dead people can also make mistakes:

— How old was he at that time?
— Seven or thereabouts.
— And what did his rabbit die of?
— Felix cried his eyes out.
— Did you see a razor at that time?
— Yes, indeed.
— And what did you think of that?
— He'd cut the rabbit open, he'd already told me that; yes, indeed, he wanted to see why it had died. . . .

As a rule I do not assume that someone watching me at billiards is watching only because he knows my life story; suddenly I become aware of it: this man is not watching the rolling ball, but just the hand, which may be the hand of a murderer, and when I look him in the face he goes back to the bar.
One gets used even to that.
Emigration would come close to a confession.

— So you say you were not perturbed when the plane landed without Jutta. You did not feel bitter that her homecoming had again been delayed? The plane was late, you say, and when you are standing at the exit and only passengers you don't know emerge, no Jutta, you were naturally somewhat disappointed. . . .

— That is correct.
— But not bitter?
— I was worried.
— What did you do then, Herr Schaad?
— I drove home.
— Right away?
— Well, I was in no hurry.
— Why did you drive to the gravel pit?
— I don't know. . . .
— You intended to go for a walk?
— I stayed in the car. . . .
— For how long?
— Later I went to the movies. . . .
— That is correct, Herr Schaad, that has been con-
  firmed; you were seen at the performance be-
  tween three and a quarter past five in the
  afternoon, in the back row on the right side, to
  be exact.
— Could be.
— What did you see at the movies?
— I've forgotten.
— Fellini.
— Could be.
— Why didn't you stay to the end?
— I thought there might be a telegram waiting at
  home, and in fact there was. I was relieved. At
  least I knew Jutta had already reached Geneva.
— You were relieved. . . .
— And that she would arrive today.

— And that was yesterday.
— Yes.
— Why did Jutta remain in Geneva?
— The plane had a scheduled stop in Geneva, I knew that, and naturally she got out after a seven-hour flight, to freshen up; I can understand that.
— Why, then, didn't she fly on?
— Because she missed the plane.
— According to the telegram.
— Yes.
— There are also trains from Geneva to Zurich.
— Jutta felt too tired for that.
— She spent the night in a hotel. . . .
— According to the telegram.
— Then why didn't Jutta call you from the hotel?

The gravel pit is no longer in operation. Grass is growing over it, there is still a conveyor belt, but rusty, likewise a notice: ENTRY PROHIBITED. And yet there is still *Nagelfluh* in abundance. A sieve lies in a brown puddle. Somewhere else a heap of gray gravel. It has not rained for two days: the tracks of my car are visible in the mud, the distinct pattern of the tires, my curve of two days ago.

— When you learned of his acquittal, Frau Schaad, you were in Kenya, waiting for rain. . . .
— That's right.

— You work in films?

— That's right.

— As a camera assistant?

— I am actually a film editor, but we are a small team, the cameraman and another man for sound, plus the ethnologist and a driver. In a small team one does everything.

— I see. . . .

— I was indispensable.

— I see.

— Of course, I was relieved when the news of the acquittal came through, you can imagine how relieved I was, I cried like a child.

— Out of relief . . .

— You can ask the team.

— You didn't feel that the acquitted might need you when he returned home after his lengthy detention and trial?

— Our shooting was behind schedule.

— And you were indispensable. . . .

— Actually, a film editor doesn't have to be present during shooting, that is true, but Herbert felt it important that I should be present from the start; that was stipulated in our contract, he wants the editor not only to see the raw footage, but also to be familiar with everything that goes on.

— Who is Herbert?

— Our cameraman.

— So the shooting was behind schedule. . . .

— We were waiting for rain.

— Without the ethnologist . . .

— Felix's two letters sounded quite cheerful, he said he was sitting in his consulting room and at last getting around to doing some reading, he was also playing billiards; yes, and I wrote him quite a long letter, too.

— About the shooting of your film . . .

— Yes.

— On your return from Kenya two days ago, Frau Schaad, did you notice anything about the acquitted when he met you at the airport?

— He was thinner.

— Anything else?

— And older; yes, I realized that.

— The acquitted maintains that you were rather shocked when you saw him standing before you, and that you only allowed him to kiss your cheek.

— I had so much luggage.

— Is it correct that he had champagne laid out at home to celebrate your reunion, and that, on this first evening two days ago, you did not wish to talk about Kenya?

— I was exhausted.

— Was that why you did not want the champagne?

— I no longer drink alcohol anyway.

— You wished to sleep. . . .

— Yes.

— Why in the guest room?

— We hadn't seen each other for a long time.

— Not since the trial.

— When Felix mentioned that he had sold his practice, I was very shocked; of course I asked him how he envisaged his future.

— What did he say?

— He shrugged his shoulders.

— And then you went to bed. . . .

— I couldn't sleep.

— Why not, Frau Schaad?

— He was sitting in the living room, I believe, drinking the champagne by himself; I heard the clock strike every hour.

— Another question, Frau Schaad.

— What will Felix do without his practice!

— Is what the acquitted surmises correct: you were afraid that being in bed together might lead to a confession, and you would suddenly find yourself lying beside a murderer?

— I am convinced of his innocence.

— So that was not the reason, Frau Schaad, for your sleeping in the guest room?

— No.

— You are convinced of his innocence. . . .

— Absolutely.

— As to last night, Frau Schaad . . .

— I kept my promise of letting him know when anything changed between us, and that is exactly what has happened.
— How did he take it?
— Chivalrously.
— As you had expected . . .
— Yes.
— And how long, Frau Schaad, has this been going on?
— I couldn't tell him in court.
— I understand.
— I also didn't want to put it in writing.
— One final question, Frau Schaad.
— Writing is so cowardly.
— What are your plans now, Frau Schaad?
— We don't know yet, it depends on whether Herbert continues in television or not.

What helps is walking.

— Now you have heard, Herr Doktor Schaad: something has changed between you and Jutta.
— I respect her frankness.
— Ten months is a long time for a woman in her mid-thirties; you were aware of that while you were in detention, Herr Schaad, and so her revelation yesterday came as no surprise. . . .
— I respect her frankness.
— Since you left your car at the gravel pit, you

have been walking for four hours, and it has begun to rain, and you have been sitting for the last half hour on a tree stump, Herr Doktor Schaad; you are not surprised, but you are wet through, and you can still think of nothing else. Is that correct?

— Yes.

— Jutta kept her promise.

— I respect her frankness.

— You've already said that.

— If anything changed between Jutta and me she would let me know—that was what she promised.

— You are shivering, Herr Schaad. . .

— I respect Jutta.

— All the same, you will catch cold, Herr Schaad, you are still sitting on this tree stump, which is damp, without a coat and without a hat, trying to hope that Jutta has in the meantime woken up and is looking for you. Is that correct?

— That is correct.

— Why don't you walk on?

What I did not see a year ago, having been in detention: the first buds on bushes here and there, furrows in the fields, black as bacon rind. The willows bordering a stream have still a reddish hue. A tractor has left black clods of earth on the asphalt, and there is a smell of manure. I avoid logging paths. At one point the boom of a jet fighter overhead. I know where I am going. Mountains in the distance, wind, probably foehn. The fruit trees are still bare, the woods transparent, above the branches one sees sky and at times, between the tree trunks, the lake, not blue, but pale, like zinc. At the edge of a pine wood there are still patches of snow in the shadow, the air is mild, an early butterfly. . . .

— When was your mother's funeral?
— Six years ago.
— Since then you have not been to Ratzwil?
— No.
— You understand why I am asking that?
— No.
— You are in your mid-fifties, Herr Doktor, and you cannot lay claim to loss of memory through age. All the things you have forgotten—isn't that strange? At the first hearing you asserted you had never actually seen the cross you once tried to use as a warning sign in the road.
— I retract my statement. . . .
— And suddenly, six years later, you remember: this cross that proved unsuitable as a warning sign, this is precisely the elaborately wrought cross on the church tower in Ratzwil, where your esteemed mother lies buried.
— It has just come back to me. . . .
— You did not forget it, Herr Doktor Schaad, you

repressed it. Like a lot of other things. All of a
sudden, while you are out walking, you have to
retract your previous statements.

— That is so.

— Doesn't that perturb you?

— Yes.

— Could it not happen, Herr Doktor Schaad, that
you might all of a sudden—for instance, while
brushing your teeth—remember where you
really spent that Saturday afternoon on which
Rosalinde Z. was strangled with a sanitary napkin in her mouth and with your blue tie, and
that you were the murderer?

What might help would be sailing.
My yawl is at the clubhouse.
I believe they are expecting me to resign.

— So you know the accused?

— As a yachtsman.

— How would you describe his character?

— Felix Schaad has admittedly always been a very
responsible yachtsman. He was less interested
in the social life of the club. . . . A doctor has
little spare time. . . . Of course, one did not
know then what one knows now, what was in
the newspapers, but I only wish to add that this
Rosalinde Z. never set foot in our clubhouse.
Never. Our guest book confirms that. . . .

I do not know how her album got into my files, which are also out of date. An album covered with blue imitation leather. Her handwriting beneath the photographs.

OUR GARDEN IN SION
ROSALINDE AT HOLY COMMUNION
OUR DOG AJAX
OUTING ON THE GORNERGRAT
WEDDING (the captain)
PALM TREES IN MAJORCA
PAPA IN MAJOR'S UNIFORM
MY INSTRUCTOR (tennis)
BEAR PITS IN BERN
REHEARSALS OF FIDELIO (the singer)
PICNIC WITH FRIENDS
IGNAZ IN HIS STUDIO (the commercial artist)
AT THE DOKUMENTA IN KASSEL
WINTER IN VIENNA (the singer)
PAPA ON A VISIT TO BERN
CRETE (the commercial artist)
SWANS NEAR ZURICH
FELIX IN HIS CONSULTING ROOM
MAMA IN THE HOSPITAL
IGNAZ AND FELIX PLAYING PING-PONG
FELIX YACHTING (twice)
MY THIRTIETH BIRTHDAY
OUR ARCHITECT (Jan)
OUR HOUSE IN ZUMIKON

The victim smiling:
as a child with dog
as a bride outside the church
as a student in Bern
as a water nymph on the beach (with harpoon)
among her family
picking mushrooms
driving a Porsche
as a guest in the Kronenhalle (Zurich)
dancing with the architect
as lady of the house (Zumikon)
mowing the lawn (ditto)

— You are Rosalinde Z.?
— Yes.
— You work as a physical therapist?

The victim smiling.

— Do you know who strangled you?

The victim smiling.

— Who, Frau Zogg, was the last person you saw in
  your life?
  . . .
— Was it Herr Doktor Schaad?
  . . .
— When he visited you on that Saturday, Frau

Zogg, it was morning, between eleven and twelve, and you drank tea together. Is that correct? Apparently it was your first meal of the day: tea and toast with pâté de foie gras. Nothing else was found in your stomach. . . . Frau Zogg, do you remember what you talked about that morning?
. . .

— When did Felix Schaad leave the apartment?
. . .

— According to the cleaning lady's testimony, the accused, your former husband, visited you regularly after you got an apartment of your own, and he knew how you earned your living. Without being shocked by it. So he claims. And you, Frau Zogg, were grateful for the assistance he gave you in tax matters. Is that correct? You regarded him as a friend, so he thinks. . . .

The victim smiling as a bride.

— Did you have a quarrel on that Saturday?

The victim smiling.

— The acquitted cannot remember what you talked about that morning. Or he is keeping it to himself. He does not even remember which dressing gown you were wearing. . . .

121

The victim smiling as lady of the house.

— In the afternoon you were wearing trousers.
    . . .
— Did anything happen, Frau Zogg, or did you say
    anything that might have upset your former
    husband to such an extent that he returned to
    the apartment three hours later to strangle you
    with his tie, or would you also confirm that the
    relationship between yourself and Felix Schaad
    was, from the time sexual intercourse ceased
    between you, a genuinely friendly and even
    harmonious one? . . . You know that Felix has
    been acquitted?

The victim smiling (with harpoon).

— Is it correct to say that, as a rule, when a visitor
    left, you locked the door to the apartment?
    And if so, who, apart from the caretaker's wife
    and Herr Doktor Schaad, possessed a key to the
    apartment on the Hornstrasse?
    . . .
— You do not wish to tell. . . .

The victim smiling as she mows the lawn.

— Were you wearing a sanitary napkin on that
    Saturday? Please pardon the question. And if

not: where could the murderer have found this soiled napkin? Presumably not in the living room, Frau Zogg, where you were discovered.

. . .

— Why did you take sleeping pills during the day?

. . .

— Presumably this was the reason you made no resistance while your feet were being bound together, or did you assume it was all part of the love play?

The victim smiling as a child.

— When he came to visit you, did Herr Doktor Schaad ever bring you flowers? And if so, were they ever lilies? The accused maintains that he dislikes lilies and has never in his life given them as a present. Can you confirm that? And if so: who on this Saturday brought or sent you the fresh lilies that were found beside the body?

The victim smiling with dog.

— As victim, you cannot be forced to make a statement, Frau Zogg, but on the other hand, a statement from you on this matter would be very helpful.

. . .

— Frau Zogg, it cannot be established with any

certainty when you took the sleeping pills. Expert evidence suggests that at four o'clock you might still have been capable of unlocking the apartment door. A witness, though admittedly a girl not yet of age, thinks she can recall seeing you later, drawing the curtains. Is that correct? We know for certain that you ate no lunch. What were you doing, Frau Zogg, up to the time of the murder?

The victim smiling as she picks mushrooms.

To come back to the tie, which you removed from the hall some time ago, after a visitor had objected to it: you knew whose tie it was?

The victim smiling as she drives a Porsche.

— Only a few of your visitors are known to the court, Frau Zogg, since for the most part they are entered in your business appointment book only by their first names and apparently did not pay by Eurocheck. . . . Was there perhaps one visitor who might have been thrown into a rage if he had discovered the accused's aforementioned tie in your green Biedermeier bedroom?

. . .

— You have understood my question?

. . .

— There is always the kind of man who falls in love even when he has to pay for it, and who consequently is unwilling to acknowledge what he in fact already knows, and is brought to earth with a thud, so to speak, when he happens on a tie belonging to another man. . . .

The victim smiling.

— Who, Frau Zogg, might fit that description?

The victim smiling among her family.

— Let me ask in another way. . . .

Drowsing is unpleasant when it produces the feeling that the van with the small barred window is waiting outside, even though I know, while still drowsing, that I have been acquitted.

— So what kind of fish was it?
— A big one.
— A pike?
— Bigger.
— And the fish was on dry land?
— Yes.
— But you say it was alive.
— Yes.
— Have you ever, Herr Doktor Schaad, heard of

a fish, no matter how big, that swallowed a snake?

— It surprised me, too.

— And what happened next?

— I watched. It was horrible; it had swallowed just half of the snake, the front half, and I saw that the fish couldn't manage any more. I saw how the snake gradually began to move again, and how the fish suddenly knew it was dying, while the snake slowly wriggled out of the dead fish. . . .

— And then you woke up?

— It was horrible.

— Herr Doktor Schaad . . .

— Horrible!

— You know what this dream means?

There is nothing left but walking.

— So you would still maintain that you parted from the victim on the best of terms?

— Yes.

— You do not feel obliged to retract that?

— No.

— When, therefore, did you recall that on that morning, while you were drinking tea together, her telephone kept ringing, and that Rosalinde got up to unplug it, and that you laughed, because it reminded you of when you were married?

— It has just come back to me.

— You did not mention it in court.

— It had slipped my memory. . . .

— On the other hand, you did mention in court that on that morning, when you went to visit Rosalinde, you saw no lilies in her apartment.

— Right.

— You do not feel obliged to retract that?

— No.

— You further maintained that you never give lilies as a present, you dislike them, you consider them tasteless. . . .

— Flamboyantly conventional.

— That is what you said, Herr Doktor, and luckily a witness, the caretaker's wife, confirmed in court that Herr Doktor Schaad, when she saw him on the stairs that morning, had brought no flowers, let alone lilies, for Madame Zogg. . . .

— That is the truth.

— You have never in your life given lilies as a present.

— That is the truth.

— You were deeply upset when you saw the police photograph, the body on the carpet, the five lilies on the body. . . .

— It was horrible.

— It was not you who gave her those lilies?

— There were often lilies there.

— You have never mentioned that. . . .

— Always five.

— Why didn't you mention that?

— I don't know. . . . -

— Your detention lasted almost ten months, Herr Schaad, the trial itself three weeks; you had plenty of time, Herr Schaad, to mention everything.

— It escaped my memory.

— And today, here in these woods, with no judge to question you, it suddenly comes into your mind: there were often lilies there.

— Always five.

— And when her telephone kept ringing, she apparently knew who was calling, which was why she unplugged it, and you laughed because it reminded you of your marriage, and when Rosalinde was in the kitchen making some more toast, you could not resist getting to your feet to glance casually at the letter that happened to be in Rosalinde's portable typewriter. Is that correct? At least you read the salutation.

— That is correct.

— How did this opening line strike you?

— As extravagant.

— Do you remember the name?

— It was a pet name. . . .

— You mentioned none of this in court—because you find it embarrassing, Herr Doktor Schaad, to admit to reading other people's letters, or what?

— It really did escape my memory.
— Because you found it embarrassing.
— What business of mine was her romance?
— It also escaped your memory that later on, after stopping for a drink on the way, you apparently got the idea of going into a flower shop and ordering five lilies to be sent. . . .
— That was a joke.
— And what time of day was that?
— No idea.
— But they were lilies. . . .
— That's right.
— Herr Doktor Schaad . . .
— That is the truth.
— What else has escaped your memory?

Of course, walking is no help, either.

— Unfortunately, Herr Schaad, what you told the police yesterday is incorrect: you did not go on foot to Ratzwil. Unfortunately, because otherwise you would not be lying in this hospital now.
— No . . .
— You drove into a tree.
— I admit that. . . .
— And the road was not at all slippery; indeed, it was not even wet. That is not correct, either, Herr Schaad, nor were there leaves lying on the

asphalt; it is summertime, you need only to open your eyes and you will see the green trees through the open window.

— How is it I wasn't walking . . . ?
— Can you feel someone holding your hand?
— Yes.
— Do you know who is holding your hand?
— A woman.
— Why don't you open your eyes?

Everything white and lacking outline and white.

— Why exactly did you drive to Ratzwil?
— It is where I was born.
— That is true, Herr Schaad, but why did it have to be the police sergeant in Ratzwil when you suddenly took it in your head to confess to the murder of Rosalinde Z.? You could have done that at any police station.
— But Ratzwil was where I happened to be.
— It is a long time since you were last in Ratzwil, Herr Schaad; indeed, you scarcely recognized the place. You made inquiries of at least two people, asking whether this was Ratzwil. In the Restaurant zum Bären, where you had a black coffee, and before it a bottle of mineral water, you told the proprietor you had come to Ratzwil on foot. Your blue car was standing outside the church.

— In the morning it was standing at the gravel pit.

— As usual when you go for a walk.

— That's right.

— Perhaps you meant to go for a walk, that may well be. Apparently you changed your mind, Herr Schaad, and returned to your car and drove to Ratzwil. Do you no longer remember that?

— All of a sudden I was in Ratzwil.

— According to the police report, you were completely sober when you reported to Sergeant Schlumpf. You were released two hours later, at exactly ten minutes past five in the afternoon, still sober. And you did not go to the Restaurant zum Bären again for a drink, or to the Restaurant zur Krone, you did not have enough time: the accident happened barely a quarter of an hour after your release from the town hall in Ratzwil, and the scene of the accident is eighteen miles outside Ratzwil, which suggests a speed of seventy-five miles per hour.

— Was it a beech tree?

— What made you drive into a tree?

— The truth and nothing but the truth.

— It was not a beech but a fir tree, Herr Doktor, no doubt about that; probably you decided to drive into a tree even earlier, somewhere you saw a linden tree maybe, then later a beech tree.

— And it was a fir tree. . . .

— Yes.

— And they were lilies. . . .

— That is an entirely different matter, Herr Schaad. . . . As for your confession: did this police sergeant have any idea what you were talking about? Or did you have to describe the murder to him in detail, the strangling with the tie, before he put the handcuffs on you?

— He found it embarrassing.

— Did he know about Rosalinde Z.?

— I didn't even notice when he put the handcuffs on me. We were at school together, Sergeant Schlumpf and I, though not in the same class: Sergeant Schlumpf is a year younger than I.

— When did you notice the handcuffs?

— Now he kept calling me Herr Doktor. If this is true, Herr Doktor, I shall have to take down a statement, Herr Doktor, if this is true, Herr Doktor, and you will have to sign the statement.

— And that is what you did. . . .

— Without the handcuffs.

— What happened then?

— I felt relieved.

— You felt relieved. . . .

— The truth and nothing but the truth.

— What were you expecting, Herr Schaad, when you were sitting there alone in the police station and noticed the handcuffs?

— I wasn't allowed to smoke. . . .

— When did you remember what you did, Herr Schaad, and in all the detail contained in this statement? The only thing you forgot was the sanitary napkin in the victim's mouth.

— Handcuffs of that sort are light. . . .

— When the police sergeant returned after a while and took you, not to a prison van, but across to the town hall and into the so-called wedding room, where the handcuffs were removed— what were you thinking as you were obliged to wait one more time?

— I had nothing left to smoke. . . .

— You remember that someone came into the wedding room to talk to you privately?

— Yes.

— That was the town clerk.

— He understood that I had nothing to smoke and offered me cigarettes; he understood nothing else.

— Do you still know what he told you?

— That my confession was false.

— You remember that?

— He hadn't even read the statement, this young man, and when I asked him to read it, he just glanced through it quickly and gave it back to me, and that was that.

— Your confession, Herr Schaad, is false.

— So he said.

— The murderer is a Greek student, his name is
Nikos Grammaticos, and he is at present being
held in the district prison.

. . .

— You must speak louder, Herr Schaad, we cannot understand, Herr Schaad, what you are
saying.

. . .

— You drove into a tree.
— And it was a fir tree!
— Herr Schaad, you might now be dead.

. . .

— Why don't you open your eyes?

. . .

— Herr Schaad, the operation was successful.

. . .

— What are you saying?

. . .

— We cannot understand, Herr Schaad, what you
are trying to say.

. . .

— Why did you make this confession?

. . .

— You are in pain.